DESIRE IN THE DEEP SOUTH

Also by Ward Greene
Cora Potts
Route 28
Ride the Nightmare

DESIRE IN THE DEEP SOUTH

WARD GREENE

CUTTING EDGE

Originally published as *Weep No More*

ISBN-13: 978-1-957868-63-9

Published by
Cutting Edge Books
PO Box 8212
Calabasas, CA 91372
www.cuttingedgebooks.com

AUTHOR'S NOTE

Life in the United States in the nineteen-twenties must seem confusing to those not old enough to have lived it as adults, which means in the year 1955 virtually everyone who is under forty.

This Prohibition Decade, this Era of Wonderful Nonsense, this Jazz Age, as it was variously called, can be remembered as one of the brightest or blackest periods in modern history.

I have heard men now sixty disagree violently on this subject. One said, exasperated by the sloth and uncertainty and delinquencies of his sons and grandsons, that in his day things were different. The young had ideals, ideas and drive; they eagerly fought a war to save democracy; returning, they pitched into work as joyfully as they did into play; they were all—well, nearly all—Horatio Alger heroes fulfilling the American success story and the American dream.

The other said, "That is a lot of hogwash. You and your friends and my friends and me never read a line of Horatio Alger. We read, for example, Sinclair Lewis. And who was he? A leading novelist of the nineteen-twenties who wrote one book attacking American culture, another deriding the American business man and a third blasting American religion. We loved him. We also loved Scott Fitzgerald, who invented the 'lost generation,' and Papa Hemingway, who wasn't papa then but an American expatriate in Paris. They were all dedicated to rebellion, rum and hell-raising, and so were the rest of us!"

This old gentleman, while speaking, was slightly in his cups, a condition that began with him in 1926, when in cups was a national habit. The novel "Weep No More," (Desire in the Deep South), published a few years later, might roughly apply to that date. In it a group of young men and women are in their cups, off and on, for a few nights and days in the fictitious city of Corinth.

The critic of the *New York Post,* reviewing "Weep No More," said it was the drunkest novel he had ever read. He did not question its accuracy. Hartford, Buffalo, Minneapolis, Sacramento and St. Louis, while noting the book's Southern locale, said it could happen anywhere. Only one city entered a denial. "Your men are not our men, Mr. Greene, and your women are not our women!" thundered the *Atlanta Constitution.* The author had not lived in Atlanta for several years then and was not aware of how things had changed.

The author hopes that this edition of "Weep No More" will show a new generation of readers a little of how things were once, (with the exception of Atlanta), in many American cities. There are no gangsters in "Weep No More," there are no millionaires, no Long Island nymphomaniacs nor Riviera wastrels. There is a lot of drinking. But there was, you know—there really was.

Rockleigh, New Jersey
June, 1955

Ward Greene

The glass was tall, tufted in green, deep with green and amber at the base and girdled by a sash of white so cold that the frost stood out in carbuncles. It was, in short, a julep as noble seeming as though the Bourbon were Kentucky's hoariest and not Miami contraband. The old head, which had reeled to fine whiskies in its day, bowed homage.

"Of course," he said, sighing, "you can't publish the facts, so why not present 'em as fiction? I don't mean merely this poor Spurlock girl's extraordinary hoax, but the facts about all of 'em. The Craycrafts; the Chapmans; the honeybee with the sting from New York; young what's-his-name in the bank; Nancy; all the old neighborhood crowd. Everybody belonged to a neighborhood crowd, once, and everybody has wondered, after he grew up, whatever happened to the old bunch? It would be interesting to tell."

He squinted at the glass as though it reflected the glories of his own youth.

"You could do it, you know," he said, "because you were brought up with them. You saw what it was like, then, in Corinth, and you see what it's like now. You know their heritage, and you know, too, that none of you would have turned out as you did—in the South or anywhere else, for that matter—if it hadn't been for automobiles and movies, and Edison and Volstead, and birth control, and radio crooners, and Elinor Glyn, and Bryan, and steam heat, and golf, and, I dare say, the world war, though I lay more hell to the man who invented lipsticks than I do to the Kaiser. Or don't you agree?

"Look at the Craycraft child. In my day, married to a cad, she would have borne her cross, taken to swooning spells and become a successful social martyr. Instead, she takes to drink when her husband takes to her girl friends and, if what they say is true, lets the modern pace versus the old ideals wreck her. Those two can't live in the same shell, apparently. Louisa Alcott and Clara Bow on a raft, so to speak.

"*Look at Nancy herself. Too much dander in her to be satisfied as a mere Southern lady. So life had her licked till the whole world went to the devil. Now I'm rather proud of Nancy. If she's a social outcast because she's married to a bootlegger—and personally, mind you, I consider Tony Bergo an excellent citizen—she's proved she can be happier pioneering her unconventional wilderness than the Craycrafts or the Chapmans tenting on their old camp ground. Not that the Chapmans aren't happy,*" he added, "*but nice people nowadays are so all-fired dull.*"

He blew into his pocket handkerchief.

"*What do you think?*" he said. "*I say you've got hold of something. Tony's a story. The modern carpetbagger, toting rum instead of swindling niggers, and destined to be our next aristocrat, I dare say. This New York smartaleck, this Eloise King, hifaluting back to her old friends to set 'em off like a pack of fire-crackers. She's a story. And what's-his-name, that woodchuck in the bank—the sallow fellow?*"

"*Fred Prentiss,*" I said.

"*Prentiss. I can never remember it. Now there's a chip off the old cavalier block! And of course, there's me.*"

He winked.

"*You'd better change names and jiggle things about a bit. You might, for instance, make me an old soak.*"

"*Where would you begin?*" I asked.

"*Why, at the beginning. Although that's too big a book. The beginning was when Adam said to Cain's oldest boy, 'Shucks, it ain't like the good old days back in Eden!'* "

So I have written the facts as fiction. I have changed the names. And instead of beginning at the beginning, I have begun the story on the Autumn evening in 1930 when Mrs. Antonio Bergo drove down from the mountains, when Eppy Spurlock told Sister Craycraft she was engaged, and when Eloise King sat in a Pullman on her way to Corinth to visit her friends, the John Ashton Chapmans.

CHAPTER ONE

A CONCRETE road, white and level in the full moon, started at the edge of the woods and stretched for almost a quarter of a mile before it curved. Not a house was near it, only red ditches on either side and beyond them peach orchards with the trees bare, and on the rolling ground beneath, a thin frost. Close to the curve, however, was an abandoned peach-packing plant, and in its shadow, at the bend, two men waited.

They leaned on motorcycles which were drawn up facing south, one behind the other, just off the concrete's edge. The men faced north, keeping in the shadow but near enough to the curve to see around it. With one step, they had an unobstructed view of the road to its vanishing point. In the moonlight, the parallel lines across the concrete showed plain—the far blot of woods, the farther smudge which was the foothills of the Blue Ridge. Over there, like the silver knob of a cane, Timbertop slept, and the feathery cloud to the right was the Nacahatchee range.

The night was very still. On the slopes, earth crumbled and ran audibly under the stools of frost. But now, as though a heart beat somewhere in Nacahatchee Valley, came a throb, imperceptible as the moon's glide at first, then sharply unmistakable through the clear air.

"Somebody comin'," said one man.

"And comin'," said the other, "like a bat outa hell!"

They acted quickly. As the roar of the oncoming motor deepened for the curve, one man shot a revolver into the air, the other pressed violently the horn on his handlebars. Brakes screeched, a car whipped around the bend, and stopped. Both men were at it like retrievers.

"Put 'em up!"—a flashlight cut a path.

It revealed a Buick sedan, all its windows closed except one through which the flash poured. Here, blinking in the glare but holding tightly to the wheel with gloved fingers, sat a woman, young, handsome and smothered in fur. She was alone in the front seat and, save for the contracted pupils of her gray eyes, apparently unflustered. Behind her, the car was a Christmas tree of luggage, bundles, sprigs of evergreen, a go-cart, toys and blankets, in the midst of which huddled a fat and aged Negress with a baby clutched to her breast. The Negress was the color of the moonlight, her eyes were white to the rims. At once she let out a caterwaul.

"Hush up, Mammy!" snapped the young woman. "It's a hold-up—but for the love of God don't wake the baby!"

She spoke into the drill of light.

"It is a hold-up, isn't it?"

No one answered—for so long that she frowned and flicked one hand as though to push the glare away.

"You might turn that damn thing somewhere else; I'm going blind!"

The light fell. She could see them now, tall, threatening—a glint of buttons—the parked motorcycles.

The young woman threw back her head and pealed laughter.

"Lordy, Mammy—I do believe it's cops! Cops! And I thought it was the James boys sure!" She relaxed across the wheel. "Listen, man, was I going too fast for you? 'Cause I just naturally can't come down from the lakes to Corinth at less'n sixty!"

Her face in the moonlight coaxed them.

"Listen here, you bound to make a case against me? Go ahead—but please, gentlemen, don't wake the baby! We just got him to sleep coming out the valley."

One man moved. Steel thumped in a holster. He said, hesitantly: "Jim?"

"Well, I dunno," said his partner. "Seems like maybe we caught the wrong rabbit." He stepped closer to the running-board. "You got any liquor in that car—lady?"

The sigh that the young woman released seemed to start at the pit of her diaphragm and to shatter through all her arteries until it expired through pouted lips.

"I have … I got one gallon of the best com liquor that ever dripped out of the still. Go on—take it! It's in that big suit-case on top. Go on, bust it up! But I hope to tell you it'll pretty near kill me—and it'll pretty near kill Major Wallace MacArthur when I get to town and tell him what happened to his corn."

The young woman moaned again.

"Mammy, what's papa going to say? What's he going to do? What's he going to do to-morrow night when the Judge and the rest of his friends come over? You know Judge Winship—you know how he despises gin—how he loathes that Jacksonville Scotch. …"

She shut her eyes tight—

"But let 'em take it—let 'em bust it up! I suppose they'll arrest us—take us to jail. Please, officer, when you get us there call up Major Wallace MacArthur, call up—"

The Negress began to wail once more, rocking the child, which had not uttered a cry.

"Hush up, Mammy!" ordered the young woman. She opened her eyes.

The law had retired a few steps to the side of the road, where a consultation was going on. In a moment, out of the shadows an arm waved.

"All right, lady—you never saw us in your life. But you better put on the brakes. Those city cops ain't so nice."

Eyes and teeth flashed in the moonlight. …

"You're lambs, both of you!" Cylinders sputtered; a red light dwindled to the south. Said Agent Boothby: "That was a damn big trunk she had on the back." Said Agent Hawes: "Nuts! I tell you she's one of them lakes people. I seen her before. The baby we want is a big wop."

In the Buick speech waited on progress. Not until the car swung up a driveway north of Corinth and stopped between a big house and a garage did a word break the rush of fifty miles. Then Mammy Pickett exploded.

"Great day in de mawnin', chile, if I didn't reckon we wuz goners! Me squattin' on forty gallons of cawn an' de jailhouse straight ahead!"

She cackled like a guinea hen.

"Chile, you sho'ly wuz cute—you fool 'em like de rabbit do de fox—Come heah, Miss Nancy! Lemme kiss you, chile!"

But the young woman had jumped out, pausing for nothing save to grasp the bundle from the Negress' arms. A back door opened, flooding the yard with light, and toward it she ran, calling as she went.

"Tony! Tony! Hello, Nipper! Down, boy, down! Here, you can have the damn thing."

She sped on, flinging out her arms.

The dog pounced where her burden hit the drive. He was a wire-haired terrier, and the rubber doll was an ancient enemy.

2

Miss Eppy Gordon Spurlock announced her engagement by the simple means of telephoning a friend she had not seen since childhood, knowing that thus would she inform all persons on Corinth likely to be interested in the miracle of romance in the life of a librarian of thirty-one.

She telephoned Mrs. Howard Craycraft, because she was prominent and had a kind heart. She had been "Sister" Meredith to every one in the old neighborhood and she was still "Sister" Craycraft to the set that gave Corinth a name for gayety among Northern visitors.

"Is that you, Sister?" said Eppy. After the exchange of exclamations the long interlude demanded, she went on in a firm voice, "I've a secret to tell you—I'm going to be married."

Whatever Sister Craycraft's surprise over the rôle of confidante thrust upon her, her response was suitably ecstatic. "Yes," said Eppy, bright but composed, "it is wonderful, isn't it? You don't know him. I met him in New York last summer, when I was studying at Columbia. His name's Jocelyn Randolph and he comes from an old Virginia family. But he's lived in New York years! Wall Street, you know."

A flush colored the lobes of Eppy's ears and strove in her pudgy cheeks as she gripped the transmitter.

"Well, not exactly poor!"—she laughed indulgently. "He has a lovely apartment in town and a place on Long Island. He says Italy for the honeymoon. What do you think?"

They talked for some time. Eppy's left ear ached, the edges of her hair were wet when at last she said reluctantly, "Well, I just thought you'd like to know, we're such old friends, Sister. Oh, I don't care, really! It's not such a *terrible* secret!"

She hung up, shaking. But her eyes, her smile were those of the conqueror. One would never have guessed that for three days she had struggled to lift the receiver.

Eppy told the family at supper. They were not as amazed as they might have been had they not observed with incredulity, amusement and finally with downright hope the arrival of letters, flowers, and candy during the three months after Eppy's return from up North. Their initial teasing had been suppressed before the hundred-to-one hazard of a wedding. With the long shot a confessed winner, the family rose and whooped.

"Well, daughter!" For a father who had prayed that a child of five be delivered from carnal thought, Mr. Spurlock's approval was more than liberal. "Well, well, well! When does the happy event come off?" Gusto was forgivable in an inquiry Mr. Spurlock long ago had mourned as among the unfulfillable.

"Oh, we haven't decided yet!" cried Eppy.

"Hooray!" yipped Joseph Moon Spurlock, himself contemplating matrimony should the roofing business ever pick up. Years of brotherhood's obligation to shunned sisterhood rang in his cheer. "Here comes the bride—ta-tah! ta-tah! When do we get a look at him? Will he build a house?"

"Oh, you'll meet him soon enough!"

Younger brother Patrick, twelve, snorted, "I'll betcha!" Since "I'll betcha!" was his verdict on all subjects, his attitude, too, could be construed as pleased. His only other comment was, "He got a car?"

"Eppy! How thrilling!" This was Sara Lee, sixteen. "I'll visit you in New York next winter! Jocelyn Randolph! He sounds simply too romantic! Mother, did you see his photograph? Could I go for him! And his letters—oh boy! Eppy, is he really rich?"

Here Mrs. Spurlock, who had been staring at her first-born as one might who beholds the ugly swan transformed into the cunning duckling, and thinking to herself that she really must have a talk with Eppy—or she could look up that copy of "What a Young Girl Should Know"—found an excuse for speech.

"Why, Sara Lee—you didn't, surely!—prying into your sister's correspondence. ... "

"Oh, hush up, Mother! Eppy doesn't care—she knew I was snooping all the time, didn't you, Eps?"

Eppy laughed merrily.

"You didn't see the important letters, anyway. They're locked up. I'll show his photograph to *all* of you!"

She sprang from the table with a toss of her head new to them, and the family, left alone, gazed at one another like conspirators after the coup. "Well, did you ever!" marveled their eyes, but their eyes smiled, too. In the next room the telephone rang, and they could hear Eppy. ... "Why, that will be wonderful! ... Next Friday? ... Oh no, we won't be married by *then*! ... Good-by, honey, and it's awfully, awfully sweet of you!" Gosh! (grinned the family) it's so! somebody else knows.

"That was Sister Craycraft," announced Eppy. Her thick lenses sparkled. "She's giving me a luncheon. . . . Now, *there's* his picture! Isn't he *gorgeous?*"

3

Sister Craycraft had decided on a party for Eppy, impulsively. She did most things on impulse, and nearly always they were gracious things. From the 'phone she walked to the front room, where the sound of a door closing had told her of her husband's homecoming. Her steps were quick, she began to hum almost before she said "good-by." Sister was always humming, and her steps were always quick—eagerness, even more than her smile and her kindness, was what her friends meant when they said, "Sister's such a good sport."

Howard Craycraft sat under a reading lamp, absorbed in his newspaper. He did not look up.

"Honey!" Sister said.

She hurried to him, a tall, fair girl fit to grace a man's home and warm a man's arms, and when he still did not look up she pushed aside the newspaper and curled herself into his lap. She gave a little unabashed grunt as she kissed him.

"Hello," said Howard. Leisurely he freed the newspaper.

"Well," he drawled, "what's new?"

"I don't know a thing. . . . How's my boy?"

"All right." Howard wiggled his knees. "Had a tough day." He wiggled his knees again. "I'd like," he said, "a drink."

Sister scrambled down. "I'll make us both one!"

Highballs before dinner were as usual in the Craycraft home and in most Corinth homes of the young and well-to-do as family prayers were in the homes of their ancestors. Concocted of corn whiskey drawn from charcoal kegs, of which the Craycrafts maintained relays of three to permit a month's "aging," they were the accepted heir of the old cocktail and the older julep. Sister's were famous for plenty of kick. One made Howard mellow, three made him jolly, vicious or dead for sleep.

While the ice tinkled above the sounds of black Lavinia's preparations for dinner, Howard flicked his trouser wrinkles and resumed Grantland Rice's column. He was a florid young man, his black hair and straight black brows like painter's strokes against his high coloring. At thirty-five, his father had been considered the handsomest man in Corinth, though even then Governor Craycraft had flaunted a statesman's proper girth. Golf had kept down Howard's waist-line, other strides of the times the desire to emulate his father's career. Let the Republicans save the country; a young man to-day goes in for politics only if he can't make money in business. Howard was content to perpetuate the family name in Dibble and Craycraft, real estate, and on the tournament and dance committees of country clubs.

"Anything on to-night?" asked Sister, returning with the highballs.

Her question was carefully casual, and so was Howard's yawn.

"I don't know. Hadn't thought about it. Why?"

"Nothing special. Thought we might get up a bridge game. Sally and Bo might like to play."

They stirred their drinks. Howard meditated on his. Sister sipped hers slowly. They seemed, sitting there, what Corinth called them: a perfect couple. Romantically they had eloped, he the Governor's son, the young officer of the first training camp detachment, cavalier of the old tradition and hellraiser of the new; she the pretty Meredith child, boyhood's forgotten "sister" suddenly and enticingly grown up. Three weeks from the day when, with new eyes, he watched her crossing the parade ground, he married her. That night they danced to the Missouri Waltz, and a month later she was to fight back tears whenever she heard the tune. "Thoroughbreds!" Corinth had applauded to the boy in France and the girl he left behind him. Sister could not have believed, then, that thirteen years could reduce their pain and ecstasy to this. "Thoroughbreds!" Corinth still applauded, seeing nothing past the falseface of the well-mannered married.

Sister thought: He will not answer. He hates the notion of an evening home. He is wishing he had not said, "I don't know." She drank half her highball—and smiled.

"This will amuse you, Howard. Guess what—Eppy Spurlock's engaged!"

"No?" Howard's relief was not altogether responsible for his sudden grin. "You mean that ugly little gal that used to live on Lee Street? My God, I'd forgotten she was alive!"

"Oh, you must remember her better than that. She had an awful crush on you when we were kids. She wasn't so ugly. Her family made her that way. Dressed her in those awful clothes and wouldn't let her go to parties without her Mother. You must remember! Her papa was a deacon or something in the Methodist church. He used to run the boys off with a whip, if they even played hiding in the Spurlock's yard. I always felt sorry for Eppy.

"Anyway," said Sister, finishing her highball, "Eppy's engaged to some fellow up North, and guess what—I'm going to give her a party!"

"Count me out," said Howard promptly.

"Oh, this will be a hen-party. A bridge luncheon, I guess. Won't it be fun if I can get all the old crowd together?"

Howard's eyebrows were darkly interrogative. "Who do you mean—old crowd?"

"Oh, you know—Sally and Ernestine Hill and all the old Lee Street bunch. A lot of them are still in Corinth. It'll be like old times." Sister swished the ice in her glass and lifted the decanter. "And Nancy MacArthur," she added as she poured.

There was nothing in the way Sister spoke this name to invest it with significance or to indicate that it had not come to her as naturally as the others, yet Howard immediately gave her a sharp glance.

After a minute, he said: "I wouldn't do that."

"What?" Sister's gaze was ingenuous. "You mean Nancy?"

"Yes—I wouldn't ask her here."

Sister laughed. "Why not? Because they bootleg? Shucks, Howard, the best people drink her stuff and I reckon that makes them just as bad in the eyes of the law. Corinth makes me a little bit tired about some folks. I always liked Nancy MacArthur. And she'd simply make the party!"

"Well, it isn't just selling liquor. You know what I mean."

Sister was looking at him with a faint pucker about her eyes. He forced himself to ignore it. "If you're talking about all that old gossip when Nancy was just a girl, aren't you a little bit silly? My goodness, the way people carry on in Corinth these days, what Nancy did was like playing cards on Sunday. I never knew exactly what she did do, anyway—it was just a lot of talk and everybody said she was a mighty cute girl till they lost their money. Money is about the same as morals around here, seems to me. You thought she was a cute girl, didn't you, Howard? By golly, I'd forgotten that!" Sister chuckled. "Was the old man afraid Old Miss was going to scare up his past?" Her eyes narrowed. "Sometimes, Howard, you're awfully quaint!"

Red-faced, Howard stirred his second highball. Sister was on her third.

"It won't be so quaint when people begin to talk about my wife running around with a damn wop. Shall we invite the Bergos to the next dinner dance at Fair Oaks?"

"Oh, Howard—you are being silly, honey. I'm not 'running around' with Nancy's husband if I invite her here. But I won't if your majesty objects. ... I'm sorry I kidded you—let's make up!"

"Well, I was just telling you how it might look," said Howard.

He kissed her, he bowed her in to dinner with traditional Craycraft gallantry, they dropped the subject of the Bergos. But

Sister could discern the little splinter still working in his vanity, she could sense the resentful and the unresolved buried between them, and all through the meal, though conversation bubbled pleasantly along, she felt depressed and baffled; highballs could cause this glow and chatter when herself, away off, struggled in vain for a lost tenderness and understanding.

Over coffee, she said: "I think I'll call up Sally about the party. You said bridge to-night was out, didn't you?"

"I'm not very keen on it," admitted Howard.

He strolled back to the living-room, where he sat with magazine and cigar. But when Sister returned from telephoning, he was not there. She could hear him in the small reception hall.

"Sally's crazy about the party. She certainly was surp—"

She stopped. Howard had on his hat.

"I'm going out for a minute. D'you mind?"

Sister did not answer. She walked slowly to the table and poured out a thimbleful of whiskey.

Howard said: "Chap leaving town to-morrow. I want to catch him, before he goes, about that Laurel Heights property. ... Say, Sister, don't you think you're hitting that stuff a little strong lately?"

She was holding up the glass, squinting through the amber away from him and she was smiling.

"It's just a grain, honey. ... D'you mind? I'd like to feel gay."

Howard stared. "I don't think that'll help you much," he drawled.

Sister put down the glass after he had gone. She began to hum the Missouri Waltz until she broke off with a little sob; then she tried diligently to cry. Her tears came hard—she had never been able to cry when most she wanted to. So she drank the drink instead.

After that she went to the telephone and called Mrs. Antonio Bergo's number and, when a negro voice replied that Mrs. Bergo was not in, left a message for her to call Mrs. Craycraft.

Howard, at the club, frowned impatiently because the line was busy. When he finally got his number, he, too, was informed Mrs. Bergo was out. But Howard did not leave his name.

4

For some time night had been impenetrable in the windows of the Sunbelt Limited, twenty hours out of New York, before it crossed the Appalachian divide and began the long drop toward the wiregrass and the Gulf. The cold dusk had given Eloise King, shivering on the observation platform, her first glimpse of mountains, and she had walked back to her Pullman wishing that she had arranged to reach this part of the journey by daylight. Already the bluffs along the roadbed were taking on a reddish hue, she had seen a cotton field with flakes still white among the black bolls, a pickaninny had waved from a tumble-down cabin, and a twinge of nostalgia swept over her. This was her land, and she was going home.

It had been a lonely, boring journey since leaving Washington. The night before there had been no time for introspection, with the gang seeing her off at the Pennsylvania Station in a dripping rain and everybody shouting and pretty well pickled after dinner at "Leo's." "Good-by, darlings! Good-by, good-by!"—and she had actually cried, hating to miss even for a month their faces and their talk, the parties they would give, her little room in the Village, Nicky's studio, "Leo's," her beloved New York with all its clamor and heartlessness. But the train itself had been an exciting novelty; soon she went to bed and slept soundly on six of Leo's old-fashioneds. In the morning, after breakfast, she had *Variety* and *The New Yorker* to read. Only with lunch, which she ate scornfully aware of the two provincials opposite, did time pall and any interest, even her fellow-passengers, become welcome.

They were an ordinary lot of travelers. Business men and their wives, salesmen, old people headed for Florida, a pair of honeymooners. Eloise had dismissed them as the sort of persons one sees coming out of the Commodore. Yet, long before the cotton fields began, she was regretting her snootiness in the ladies' washroom, she was eavesdropping on conversations, she was developing a queer sense of timidity. Southerners were in the majority on the train, obvious by their accent, and Eloise's feeling was strange because though she herself had been born and raised, as she said, in Corinth and, though her New York friends kidded and flattered her about her own accent, she always moaned, "Oh, my God!" when Southerners were mentioned.

Eloise had lived in New York ten years. She did not say "Oh, my God!" about the South; indeed, she defended the South frequently and hotly and had been known, at studio teas, to argue the righteousness of lynching and Tom Heflin, though she was not sure exactly who he was. The South was a right and beautiful legend to Eloise, and so were Southerners in the abstract. Only when they visited New York and got drunk, tried to rape you in taxi cabs, wanted to go to Harlem and brawled when they did, yelled the rebel yell on Broadway, cursed publicly the plague of Jews, asked how you stood the life and said they wouldn't have New York if you gave them the place, only whenever she had to encounter a Southern friend in the flesh did Eloise shudder.

Sally Chapman and her husband, for example, had been a trial. Of course, they weren't the objectionable kind of Southerner, they were nice people, they stopped at the Plaza, they wanted to see plays instead of musical comedies. Bo was good-looking and Sally was charming in her slow, innocent way. It would have been better, perhaps, if they had been the other kind. She and Arthur—she had been living with Arthur then—had talked it over and agreed that Eloise must do something for her friends. That was after Bo had taken them all to *The Green Pastures* and Texas Guinan's, after Eloise had been Sally's guest at luncheon and a matinée. Of course, Eloise didn't feel any real sense of obligation—when you give out-of-towners the benefit of your companionship and your knowledge of New York, you practically square accounts. Besides, the Chapmans were well off—they'd come to New York to blow their money, hadn't they?—neither she, who wasn't "working" then (as we say in show business), nor Arthur, an impecunious painter, could afford the Broadway idea. Out-of-towners shouldn't expect it.

So they gave Sally and Bo a party in the Village. Or rather, because it wouldn't have done to have the Chapmans at Arthur's place, they persuaded a friend to give one of her studio parties at which a lot of artists and writers were sure to be, and they invited Sally and Bo. As Eloise said to Arthur afterward, if the Chapmans had a dull time—well, it was their own fault for being dull people. Not many Corinth visitors are lucky enough to meet persons like Mars Maxwell and Aaron Heim, and if the Chapmans didn't know what a humanist was and hadn't read Heim's novels, well, at least they might have pretended and not departed at the moment Mars was discussing homosexuality so interestingly. It had looked so bigoted and stupid—my stars! when you're in Rome do as the Romans. "Anyway, they're off your conscience," said Arthur, and Eloise said, "Yes, thank heavens! But if I ever have to entertain any more Southerners—!"

Nevertheless, she was delighted six months later to receive a prompt answer to her letter to Sally. Arthur had gone to Paris in June, and the summer had been wretched. Even the best illustrators were not hiring models, and by October Eloise was reduced to occasional posing for commercial photographers.

"I am waiting on a new play Al Woods is putting on," she had written Sally. "It's a lovely thing! and the part he has for me is so amusing I've turned down a number of other producers. But rehearsals won't start for a month yet, hence, at the moment, I'm bored. I've decided to run away—guess where?—to little ole Corinth! I suppose I should stay with Aunt Charlotte, but the poor old thing has so little room that, much as I know she wants me, I shall probably go to a hotel. Wretched solution, I know, but one does hate to impose." Sally's response had been perfect: "We couldn't think of your staying at a hotel! We have a big house—loads of room—and if you don't mind putting up with the children. ... Wire what train you are catching. ... "

And so she was on her way to Corinth, which she hadn't seen in ten years, and a little thrilled by the prospect, and a little disquieted because people in a Pullman spoke a familiar accent with an assurance outlanders had no right to.

The Pullman seemed to belong to these people, the train, the lazy-bright land into which it bored. A little while ago she had gone into the club car to smoke a cigarette, and she had heard a man say, "New York? I wouldn't live there if you gave me the place"—and she had not smiled, she had been uneasy, she had felt that men were staring at her, and she had put out her cigarette and returned to her section. Outside her window she could see a long white road; the moon was up now, the mountains were close and wrapped in silver.

What would Corinth be like? What would the Chapmans, who had seemed so dull in New York, be like in their own home? And all the others whom she had not seen in ten—fifteen—some even in twenty years? For when the old crowd on Lee Street began to break up, its children had gone east and west, to other parts of the city, away to school and away on vacations. She herself had gone away to school and then to her step-mother's home in Cincinnati, and returned to Corinth infrequently, keeping up with only a few old friends such as Sally, and all but dropping those after New York.

Eloise thought of Lee Street.

Little girls in "middy blouses" and pleated skirts walked, arms twined and six abreast, through spring twilight, singing "School Days" and "The Good Old Summer Time," giggling, whispering, envying their elder sisters' silk petticoats and pompadours and beaux who brought them candy and books illumined by the goddesses of Gibson and Fisher and Howard Chandler Christy.

Those little girls saw sex only as John Drew in a tuxedo or romantic strangers making princely love to Beverly of Graustark. They despised grubby little boys, running grubbily in the dusk, and chirped "23 for you—skid-doo!" to their taunts. And though, later, they learned with those little boys the "one-step" and the "hesitation waltz," and let them wear "seal" rings, and held their hands, breathlessly, in dark nickelodeons, there were no kisses, though moonshade and wisteria veiled the porch, only a pulse in the young breast and a clean wish—"Starlight, star bright!"—flung to the clean night and the unpredictable years.

Eloise shrugged her shoulders. We were little saps, she thought. Sally and Sister Meredith and Nancy MacArthur, the Hill girl and the funny child who wore high boots and cried when you teased her about boys; what was her name? Eppy something. "Eppy, Eppy, stick, stax steppy, E-legged, I-legged, bow-legged Eppy!" I wonder whatever became of her? ... and of Sister and Nancy and the others. ... Funny what happens to people. Funny what happened to me—Nicky, Arthur and all that. What would they think of me in Corinth if they knew? ... And what would you care what they thought? At least you have lived. ... In Corinth they do not know what living is!

Eloise smiled defiantly at the moonlit road, where a Buick sedan kept pace madly with the Sunbelt. The train was slackening speed, and when she put her face close to the pane, she could distinguish a glare in the west.

"Corinth in ten minutes, ma'am!" announced the porter.

She allowed him to brush her, oddly glad of his subservience, and when he took her bags, she gave him a dollar, a proper tip for a New Yorker and one, she believed, bigger than the tips those other passengers gave.

A bewildering station ... strangers, strangers, Sally and Bo ....

"Hi, there! Hi, there!" they shouted.

"You darlings!" cried Eloise.

5

To a group marsheled around bottles in the kitchen, Nancy Bergo vividly described high adventure on the Blue Ridge road. ... In her room, Sister Craycraft slept, her breathing heavy, her clothes wherever she had dropped them ... and in hers Eppy Spurlock sat before her mirror, writing.

On Eppy's dressing-table was the portrait she had shown the family—almost theatrically handsome, the chin cleft, the eyes luminous under the pale forehead with its slash of black hair. But Eppy did not gaze at the portrait, she gazed at her reflection, and her own eyes, bracketed though they were by tortoise-shell, shone not less luminously.

"My beloved," she wrote in a cramped, tortuous script, "I am not lonely to-night. The moon is a witch. She is Astarte and Cytherea, with a magic over mortals to swing them together as she swings the tides. You are here, beloved, closer than breath, sharper to the sense than fire or rose or symphony. ... "

CHAPTER TWO

BREAKFAST WITH the Bergos was apt to be an affair as lavish, if not as formal, as dinner in the homes of the ordinary rich, depending on the quantity, nationality, appetite and social whims of those breakfasting, who might be merely the members of the Bergo household or might include guests and retainers unrestricted as to number, color or caste.

Even on quiet mornings, when the household alone was to be fed, considerable bustle began from the moment the master of the house, Mr. Antonio Bergo, respectively of Milan, Bleecker Street, Hell's Kitchen, Broadway, Miami Beach and Corinth, descended at seven o'clock. Saluting him on the buffet were fruits, oatmeal porridge, marmalade, crumpets and tea—a menu he had embraced after business trips to the British West Indies, and one in which his wife, Nancy, indulged him along with his affection for matched haberdashery, bogus works of art, unreasoning bursts of charity and any sort of game on which he could bet. Tony was an immense, rocky man with gray eyes and a baby's complexion. He smiled constantly but apologetically, as though all jokes were on himself. At breakfast he wore one of his nineteen bathrobes and ate standing, chatting with the cook if no other companionship offered. After every meal he used a finger-bowl.

Unless the night before had been too strenuous, Nancy soon joined him. Her wants were simple, orange juice and black coffee. They were served her in the sunny alcove of the dining-room, where Mrs. Bergo propped herself in the window-seat and read the morning paper ... but not for long. Other breakfasts eclipsed hers.

Upstairs, in the spare bedroom, one of the young bloods from the University might be waking to complete perplexity regarding his whereabouts and to a condition of nerves only bromides and a double whiskey sour could subdue. The Bergos would prescribe. Or, if it was not one or more collegiates, it might be the collegiates' elder brothers staggered in from the poker game at the Athletic Club—in any case, the Bergos to the rescue. Occasionally the spare bedroom sheltered sisters of the bloods, or young ladies of no kin whatever to the gentlemen, in which event the latter were exiled to the sleeping porch or bedded down on distant couches. For, in Mrs. Nancy Bergo's words, "I'm a plain bootlegger—if you two turtledoves can't resist the nesting impulse, you'll have to find another tree. Come on—break!—or trot out of here!"

Whether the Bergo hospitality consoled the local sybarites, or merely cronies of Major MacArthur's enticed overlong by the redeye, or some of those visiting gentlemen—swarthy, furtive and courteous—who now and then drove up in their limousines from Florida to confer mysteriously with Tony, all must be breakfasted and each could be confident of receiving the breakfast of his choice, be this whiskey, ham and eggs or salami.

Infrequently, when the press of guests beneath the Bergo roof approached the size and variety of a circus troupe, mutters of irritation rose from the kitchen where Mammy Pickett perspired. But at its liveliest a Bergo breakfast was an affair of savor, babble and reviving spirits, with the hosts solicitous at the bedside or moving hearteningly among those able to achieve the descent; and if, with laments above, trays banging on the stairs, racket in the dining-room, uproar in the kitchen and Nipper, the dog, racing between everybody's legs, the effect was dinny, it was also cheerful; remorse retreated, paying customers forgot both their sins and their resolutions and, as Tony Bergo said, squinting at forty acres of verdure, "Nature ain't bad—no noisy neighbors driving you nuts."

On the morning of November eleventh, the Bergos were comparatively solitary. Mr. Bergo finished his crumpets alone. Drying his wet nails on the handkerchief that flamed above his robe of dark blue corduroy, he hastened to the front lawn of "The Shack." His skirts billowed, his crimson ankles sparkled over the frosty turf, for Mr. Bergo pursued a duty paramount at the moment to his integrity as a host or a husband. In a regimental history of the Eighty-Second Division, the name of Corporal A. Bergo appears briefly but gloriously, and though the Corporal had lived to defy the government he had defended, Armistice Day invariably saw him pay it homage in the manner of a true patriot.

On a rise a short distance from the Bergo gate, a flagpole stuck its nose toward the sky, and here awaited Corporal Bergo the colored boy, Skeet, hired more for his talent on the mouth organ than his skill as a gardener. In Skeet's right hand was a bugle, across his left arm rippled a flag which he handed ceremoniously to Corporal Bergo. Ensued, since the silk had not kissed the breeze since July Fourth, some discussion as to mechanics before the flag was finally tied and run up to the peak, whereupon Corporal Bergo, his robe flapping but his back a rod, stood at salute while Skeet trumpeted loudly and amorously into the sunrise.

Out to them, at the conclusion of this rite, sauntered Major Wallace MacArthur in dark gray morning coat, striped trousers, gray spats over highly polished shoes, with a pearl pin in his black ascot tie, a geranium in his buttonhole and what used to be known as a "planter's hat" on his silvery head. The Major, who considered his son-in-law a sartorial Zulu, had not varied this costume for prize-fight or church in forty years.

Presently, having instructed Mammy Pickett, he would return to the house for a proper breakfast of omelette, coffee, waffles and cane syrup, with a pony of Bourbon as an apéritif and a second pony by way of digestant. Presently, then, should no motor be available, he would stroll the dozen blocks to the street car line, to be transported at a cost of five cents to his daily round of duties and pleasures. Of the latter, time had been when the Major yielded to no man his choice and his zest for them; but the arts and the arteries having fallen on evil days, the Major would be content to establish himself, were the weather kind, in a chair outside the Cherokee Hotel or, did cold or rain smite, on a divan in the hotel's peacock alley. Here, so distinguished a landmark that the management would have deplored his loss, he would gaze for hours on the Corinth comedy, bowing to acquaintances, chuckling with a gossipy friend, his geranium ever fresh, not a hair of his mustache out of place, but his nostrils twitching, his watery little eyes lighting up, and these unfailingly when luck brought upon his stage a pretty woman (the younger the wider the Major's nostrils twitched), the approaching cyprian or vestal inescapably aware of the attention she drew and of the fine old gallant or the nasty old man, according as she judged life. Simple—the latterday recreation of the Major—but who shall say what vicarious conquests, what beauties resurgent warmed his scalp?

Of the duties of the Major, but one was vital and this, fortunately, often could be blended with pleasure. The Major was looked to by his daughter and son-in-law to be their ambassador to trouble. During his career he had been farm-boy, soldier, barkeep, liquor dealer, real estate agent, stock-promoter and, for a period, Miami millionaire; but, better than these, he had been a police commissioner of Corinth from 1895 to 1915, and though his régime had gone out with the old bad days of the brothel, the saloon and the crap-joint, the Major's influence remained. He had friends in high places, and an ear to the very low ground. The members of the force he knew by name, and the names of their wives and children; the Chief himself did not pass the Cherokee without a salute to the Major; and, for the rest, the Major had a beat like any patrolman—the hotel, the courthouse, the city hall—if duty did not come to the Major's chair, he sighed and conscientiously trod it out.

The Major was worth a salary. Due to his vinous habits and the sternness of his daughter, who both loved him and valued him as a business asset, he received none. Hence his presence on the lawn in the chilly November morning. In his pocket was fifty cents, bestowed with a lecture by Nancy; and in his mind's eye, as he approached Tony, a vision of that barroom opposite the police station.

"A glorious day, Tony—my respects to you and the colors!"

The Major included both in his wave—with a wink for Skeet, not to be forgotten as a dependable cup-bearer in time of censorship.

"Chief—good morning," beamed Tony. He admired his father-in-law just as he admired, with whole soul, anything belonging to Nancy, and he was always deferential to the old gentleman. He said now, being proud of his old-fashioned Americanisms, "You're an oily boid, sir."

The Major nodded abstractedly; there were occasions, he confessed, when modern slang baffled him. Fixing his eyes on Tony's deep blue shirt, he considered a dignified opening for his mission.

"Family up, sir?" inquired Tony.

"Nancy's awake, but she's not down yet. Young man in the spare bedroom—name Prentiss, Pennies, something of the sort—still asleep.... That's a nobby tie-clasp, Tony."

His son-in-law gazed down where ruby flashes broke the swell of chest. "Just cluck stuff," he declared. "Took it off a guy in Atlantic City in a dice game. Knew it was a phony when I faded him, but he was a sweet guy.... You like it, Chief? Here—"

The Major, who abhorred tie-clasps and who had spoken simply on the theory that compliments often pave the way to cash, nevertheless accepted the bauble graciously. After all, cyprians sometimes pause—and the ladies, one learned long ago, appreciate trinkets of any sort.

"As a matter of fact, Tony," he plunged, "I was thinking of purchasing a clasp. A clasp and a number of other trifles. But I'm a little short just now ... a little short .... Shirts, too, I'm a bit low on shirts"—he had, to Tony's knowledge, thirty never yet used. "I wonder, my boy, if you could spare a small loan?"

As Tony's hand dug, he and the Major simultaneously performed a maneuver like an act rehearsed. This consisted of a shift by the Major to the right and a shift by Tony to the left, bringing them into a parallel line with the house, the Major nearest it; in effect, the Major stymied Tony. At the same instant, Tony raised wary eyes towards a front window. During this pantomime, a bill exchanged hands.

"Okay, Chief?"

"Okay, my boy.... Very generous of you ... gentleman's accommodation ... matter between you and me, am I right, sir?"

They moved across the lawn, the Major's hand affectionately under his son-in-law's, the latter striding with chest high and his apparel flaunting brilliance equal to the flag's they left. Towards this, as their voices retreated, Skeet cast eyeballs and a chuckle.

"Flag," he said, "you an' me got some boss!"

2

In a dressing jacket bright among pillows—beautiful, he thought, as a red-headed angel among tombs—Antonio Bergo's wife drank coffee and smoked.

"I'm being lazy," she announced. "D'you mind, Tony?"

He sat on the edge of the bed and locked his hands around her upright knees. "Nancy, baby, I don't mind if you stay right there forever."

"Tony! Is that nice?" She hunched over to give him more room. "An invalid or a trollop, I suppose. But I'm sure you don't want me to be an invalid.... Do you want me to be a trollop, Tony?"

Letting her kid him—he got a kick out of that. He said, sternly: "I wish you wouldn't say that—'trollop.' It sounds lousy. Know what I mean? I mean you can do any damn thing you want to—except like another guy. If you ever like another guy, I'll...."

"Yes, darling! What?"

"I'll eat your ear!" finished Mr. Bergo, grimly.

She wilted among the pillows. "Is that all! Tony, can I never reform you? ... Just a big wop! Just a big, tough gorilla...."

After that they gazed at each other for several minutes.

He was as inexplicable to her as ever. As inexplicable, as uncouth and as lovely as the day he marched onto the beach at La Playa in black trunks, cherry shirt and a green and yellow béret. Between her and the Caribbean, where the sunset flung depressing beauty, stalked Hercules in motley; she sat up and forgot, for the first time in weeks, what a sewer life can be at twenty-four. "I know him," said the man with her, "but don't tell your friends at the Sevilla who introduced you!" It was not, she kept thinking that night, because he was big or good-looking or so unapologetically roughneck that he touched her; nor was it his careless gambling at the Jockey Club; nor his good manners at dinner, nor his skill in the *danzon*. It was, she decided near dawn, because she was intoxicated yet unkissed—the sensation, not the man, was refreshing. Later, in Miami, and still unkissed after nights of Cuban moonshine and days of intimate sun, she knew better—it was the man. One does not listen, kissless, to hours of boyish confession in thug's lingo without discovering that one is worshiped and—admit it!—worshiping. Not when one celebrated a war at eighteen and learned in its hangover to feed a fever lest it die. Perhaps, indeed, he got her on the rebound from satiation; whatever the case, she loved him.... Dad, who should have raged, waited until after the elopement to mention that the Florida "boom" had bankrupted him. And that, she felt, was damn decent of Dad; the cats in Corinth, who would say it anyway, could not say truthfully that she had married her wop for his money.

"Why did I marry you, Tony? Why did you marry me?"

He wriggled under her lazy inspection.

"Aw, kid, lay off. Always askin' 'why—why'—what's it matter why a thing happened? Ain't it good enough I love you without I got to give you blueprints? I married you because you're a swell kid. Why you married me, I dunno any more'n who killed Rot'stein."

She smiled. "That's fair enough ... I'll tell you why I married you, Tony. I married you for your beautiful ears. They look just like cunning little pin-cushions, dear. ... How'd you grow them?"

He jerked away—no need he should drag up those "Battling" Bergo days; Jeez 'n' Christ, hadn't she enough to be ashamed of about him?

"Hey, quit that! I won 'em in a raffle. Listen, Nancy, you got some 'phone calls. ... Lemme see. ... Didn't tell you last night I got so steamed up hearin' about those bulls. ... Mrs. Howard Craycraft says call her."

Mrs. Bergo blew meditative smoke. "I wonder what she wants? I haven't seen Sister in years. Maybe it's liquor for Howard."

"He the guy out here last week with Prentiss?"

"Yes."

"Nice guy," said Mr. Bergo, placidly.

Mrs. Bergo studied him. "He's not. And you don't think so. Oh, he's all right, I suppose, if he wasn't so pretty and didn't know it."

"I thought he was a sweet guy."

"Ummmmm—I saw you being nice to him—he's an old friend of mine, you know."

"Yeh?" said Mr. Bergo, innocently.

" 'Yeh,' " mimicked Mrs. Bergo. She added, still studying him, "I had an affair with him once, when I was a kid."

Mr. Bergo leaned over and adjusted the seam of his right sock. He appeared not to have heard; he yawned. Then he got up and tapped a cigarette and strolled toward the door.

"Tony," said Mrs. Bergo, "come back here."

He came back, pink under his simulated surprise, and Mrs. Bergo laced fingers behind his neck.

"Tony, I never want you to feel. ... "

"Listen, kid," he broke out, "you didn't have to tell me that. Why, Jeez 'n' Christ, didn't I know it minute he come in here, way he acted? That guy's a no-good guy. But I can't blame him for fallin' for you, Nancy. ... You don't have to tell me things like that, baby!"

"But I didn't want ...."

She checked herself, staring at him. "You're sweet, Tony."

"Okay, kid. ... Now I'll bring the books, that's what I was goin' for," said Mr. Bergo.

3

Fred Prentiss was not happy in the Bergos' automobile.

Fred had not been one of the old Lee Street crowd. He had been brought up on the undistinguished south side of Corinth, in a neighborhood of laborers' sons and the children of small tradespeople. But in high school he had begun to "run with" fellows like Bo Chapman and Howard Craycraft, assiduous to win their tolerance, and they had invited him to some of the North Side dances where, by industrious attention to homely girls and to mothers, he had achieved a sort of popularity. Eventually this had led him into society and a job in the Third National Bank; he dressed well, cultivated the right acquaintances, joined a club and, during the war, drew the notice of important people by his zeal for the Liberty Loans and the Red Cross. His mother still "took in sewing" of mechanics' and grocers' wives; she was very proud of Fred, who saw her seldom and in his own world passed for an orphan as well as a bachelor.

Fred's career had given him an easy manner yet left him memories, half servile and half resentful, that occasionally made little blisters in his outward assurance. Thus, with most members of the old Lee Street crowd he could chatter, with a sprinkle of "Do-you-remember's" and "That-was-the-night's," in a way to convince them that he had "belonged" always and only their stupidity was at fault for failure to recall him in rompers. But when the old Lee Streeter was Mrs. Antonio Bergo, and their chat was public, Fred teetered unhappily. Here was anomaly: with Nancy MacArthur he had been proud and glad to strut as an equal; with Nancy Bergo he felt very much the seamstress's son whose social prestige could not risk gossip linking him with bootleggers.

Seated beside her in the back of the automobile this brisk morning, Fred eagerly, at first, swapped reminiscences of Eppy Spurlock. He was vain of the fact that he had known Eppy, had actually escorted her to parties. When Nancy had come from telephoning Sister Craycraft with the news of Eppy's engagement, Fred had jumped right in with personal memoranda.

"Say," he bragged as Tony steered the Lincoln into the highway, "did you know the Spurlocks used to keep watch on Eppy like she was in a convent or something? Sure! They wouldn't let her have company till she was sixteen years old, and then the old man or the old lady always sat in the next room with the door open. They sure were foolish if they thought anybody was going to make a pass at Eppy! 'Course I only went out there two or three times—felt sort of sorry for her—but one night I remember we were sitting on the front porch and I just put my arm on the back of the swing, like that, and Eppy gave a little jump and grabbed me and kind of pointed and, sure enough, there was the shadow of somebody standing behind the front door, and Eppy gasped, 'Don't!—Don't do that!—It's papa!'—Did I snatch myself away? Boy!—And how!"

Fred cackled loudly, the genial raconteur, yet each moment, while he was telling his story, his sense of disquiet grew.

The car, a hunter's green and gleaming with silver and nickel, had swung into Cherokee Road and was booming the ten miles to Corinth. The top was down. Tony, with his hat off and the wind wrenching his crimson tie from his fawn great-coat, looked like an advertisement in *Vanity Fair* Major MacArthur, next to him, invited notice in his own fashion; he might have been a capitalist rushing to merge six more railroads. Nancy's choice of hats had not been funereal and, altogether, the Bergo ensemble was provocative of more than a glance.

This early in the morning—it was not yet eight when Fred, with some misery, had managed the Bergos' shower and a cup of coffee—traffic was not heavy on Cherokee Road, but what there was of it included motors as splendid as the Lincoln; Packards, Cadillacs, Chryslers, they passed and were passed by Tony as they rolled from driveways serving the mansions on the hills. The lords of Corinth keep pioneer office hours, the masters rise with the slaves, and many a Corinth wife, her sables flung over a housedress, drives her man to work and has concluded her marketing before ten o'clock. Hence the Lincoln soon was part of a procession increasing in magnificence and diminishing in speed as the skyline of the city bourgeoned.

Fred Prentiss had not planned a morning spin with the Bergos—his intentions, in fact, had included them not at all when he got into the poker game at the club the night before—but, with a headache, no money and the office fifteen miles away, he had been grateful when Tony offered a lift to town. Now he regretted; he might have 'phoned the bank he was ill; a limousine roared abreast and Fred cringed.

"Cold?" asked Nancy.

"I feel rotten. Helluva hangover."

"If you're going to be sick," said Nancy practically, "just hang your head over the side. You won't hurt the Dabneys' Rolls—it isn't close enough. Better take your hat off, anyway; wind'll do you good."

Fred removed the hat, hastily put it on again as the Lincoln nuzzled a street car, and muttered something about pneumonia.

"Nonsense," said Nancy, "not in this weather. Tell you what, Freddie, we'll stop at that drugstore across from the bank and get you a bromo."

"I don't think...I guess, Nancy, I better *not* go straight to the bank...even if I'm late, better go home and change my clothes.... Look here, you might put me down right here!"

"Tony"—the Lincoln slowed—"Fred wants us to drop him, he's not feeling well."

They commiserated with Fred as he crawled out; they offered to run him the few blocks off the main thoroughfare to his flat; Tony detained him with special recipes for that jumpy feeling. And Corinth trundled past. ...

"And that's that," said Nancy. "The worm!"

"What hit him all of a sudden?" inquired Tony. "I thought he was all jake the way you and him was fannin' about the good old days. I like to hear about when you was a kid, Nancy. That Mrs. Craycraft want anything?"

"Oh, Freddie broke out with social eczema. He was afraid we might scrape a Colonial Dame's bumpers—how I'd like to! No, she didn't want anything much. She's giving a luncheon for this Spurlock girl and she asked me. Why, I can't imagine. By Jinks, I'll be damned if I'll go! They give me a slight attack of hydrophobia, the Corinth ladies' auxiliary of the mentally unemployed.... But Sister's a nice girl."

Major MacArthur, batting his watery little eyes, never seemed to be the serpent protecting its young. He merely batted and struck.

"She was a Meredith, wasn't she, daughter? Ah, I remember...Jack Meredith...grandfather...no, this girl's father's uncle. Ran a quarry out by Tuckertown till he shot that fellow … what was his name? … Simpson … Simpkins. … H-m-m-m … nasty business … in the back … family hushed it up … got off with man-slaughter. … But people talked."

"Well, Sister's a nice girl, anyway. She didn't pick her ancestors."

"Lovely child," agreed the Major. "I remember her well. When her father was in financial difficulties in 1900, he came to me. …"

The Major's memory was deadly enough to embarrass half the first families of Corinth, a weapon which he felt his daughter sometimes did not sufficiently utilize. His voice fluted on and Tony, listening, swung the Lincoln ahead with mild wonder in his smile. Try and tie 'em, these Southerners! You'd never think, till somebody like the Major blew their top, the dopes and heels they had in their families along with the class. Always he'd had a yen for the South, from his conscription into the training camp near Corinth in 1917; one reason he had gone for Nancy was because she was a Corinth girl, and you bet he had liked the idea of shifting the business there. He still adored the South, the Major's yarns were merely a whet to his delight in being a Corinthian among the Corinthians. But a faint frown began to cloud his smile.

"Nancy, honey," he said when the Major paused, "don't you want to go to Mrs. Craycraft's party?"

"What?" She had been inattentive for blocks.

"Mrs. Craycraft's party. You ought not to pass it up. Ain't I right, Chief? All your old friends'll be there. You don't see 'em much. You'd get a kick out of it."

"Oh, I don't know. Maybe I'll go. … Listen, Tony, Prentiss pay you last night?"

"Nope."

"He didn't? The little cheater! What's he owe now?"

Tony, with one hand, expertly consulted a notebook. "Forty-six dollars."

"And he's owed most of it months! Dad, do you reckon—?"

The Major caressed his mustache. Water misted his gaze, but the vision he beheld was clear enough. Scene, the interior of the Third National Bank. The Major has dropped by to pass the time of day with his old sidekick, Tom Whipple, first vice-president. As they talk, it is natural that they should be observed by the bank's employees, including a certain young teller, and if, from the Major's manner, this one should suspect sinister intentions of which the Major was completely innocent. . . .

"Don't worry, daughter," said the Major, "I'll get the money. By the by, I can't seem to recall that young man's family at all. Pennice? Pennies?"

4

Nancy had finished her shopping, even to wave and manicure at the beauty parlor, and it was not yet twelve o'clock. She had nearly an hour before Tony was to meet her with the car, and she was bored. She could, like most housewives she knew, consume the hour in a department store, or she could, like their younger sisters, spend it on the street. The stores would be acluck with the housewives pawing everything from clothes-pins to fur coats, and Cherokee Avenue would be blooming with pretty girls, parading past the soda founts where the business man sacrificed to Coca Cola and optically sinned. Nancy detested Corinth's housewives, maidens, men and their pastimes.

She wished she were a man. If she were a man, she could just loaf, she could join the Major in the sun before the Cherokee Hotel, she could smoke and spit and tell dirty stories in comfort and propriety. Too bad Corinth didn't have sidewalk cafés. It would be pleasant to kill an hour at Sloppy Joe's. . . . Suddenly an idea kindled. Ahead was a huge bulk of granite she had not visited in years, the Carnegie Library—she would go in and find Eppy Spurlock and wish her luck!

Miss Spurlock, said the attendant, was on the third floor in the "restricted room," a phrase which nonplused Nancy until a favorite yarn of the Major's recurred to her.

"You don't remember when the city had its own library, do you?" the Major would say. "It was in that little, old red building where the Courthouse is now, and I reckon it was the doggonedest collection of books you ever saw jostled together anywhere. Well, when Mr. Carnegie began pitching libraries to the boys and Corinth grabbed one, I was on the committee that took stock of our assets and merged them with the new foundation. The records of our old library listed, among other things, a Burton's 'Arabian Nights' which old man Charteris gave the city when he died and which his son said was quite rare, very valuable and, of course, unexpurgated. But, though the books were on the records, they weren't on the shelves. Who stole Burton? Nobody knew till somebody thought to mention the matter to Miss Netty Sparks, the head librarian. You remember Miss Netty—they used to say she ate green persimmons for breakfast. Well, Miss Netty was flustered, but she solved the mystery. 'I burned those books,' she said. '*Burned,* Madam?' said old Pete Golightly. 'But, Godfrey Mighty, they are valued here at more than five hundred dollars!'—'I don't care,' said Miss Netty, 'I would sooner see the young people of Corinth dead and in their graves than exposed to such filth!' We daren't say another word, but we did insist on no more bonfires; we set up a restricted room for books Miss Netty couldn't stand but the incorruptible and the hopelessly damned might want to read, and old Pete Golightly, who never had read a book in his life, sneaked out that afternoon and bought the 'Arabian Nights.' He never spoke to Miss Netty again. They sold him, of course, a regular children's edition."

That Eppy Spurlock, remembered as a disciple of Louisa Alcott and the "Little Colonel" books, should evolve into the landlady of a bibliothetic red light, struck Nancy as incredible. Did Eppy, in whose home Nancy once had quailed for daring to mention "Three Weeks," actually read D. H. Lawrence? Did she, no doubt, know Proust and forbid him to flappers who knew birth control? Eppy had been a smart girl ih school, one might have pictured her as a missionary teaching trigonometry to the heathen Fiji—but never as Madam Erotica trotting out call-books, as it were, for the carriage trade! Nancy paused on the threshold of the "restricted room" with a jest crowding congratulations from her lips.

"I beg your pardon—have you 'Lady Chatterley's Lover'?"

"No, indeed—the library does not keep suppressed books!"

The spectacles raised above the desk glinted icily.

"Well, you ought to read it, Eppy—it's hot stuff!"

"I have—"

In her surprise, Eppy was on the brink of confessing that a locked shelf in her bedroom held the tall, black volume. She gasped, blinked and cried, "Why, Nancy MacArthur, what on earth are *you* doing here?"

"Can't I find out about the facts of life as well as the rest of Corinth? Or am I too young? Don't be all hot and bothered, Eppy—honest, I really dropped in to felicitate you—I think it's swell you're engaged!"

"Why … Nancy! … that's awfully, awfully sweet of you! … But how'd you *know*? How'd you find *out*? I haven't told a soul but the family and, well, a *few* close friends. … Oh, I can guess! Sister Craycraft told you, didn't she? My goodness, the way things get around in this town! I never dreamed … but it *is* so sweet of you … coming in like this … and you'll be at Sister's luncheon, of course! Isn't it *terribly* sweet she's giving me a luncheon?"

The decision to call on Eppy had been as much whim as good-heartedness. Nancy had not anticipated an emotional flood, this blushing and fluttering and ardor for her to come in and sit down, nor did she exactly relish it … having to look at Eppy, tubbier and frumpier than she was fifteen years ago; having to listen to Eppy's gush about her fiancé, his looks, his family, his wealth; having to prod Eppy with expected questions so that Eppy might play coy. Nancy felt embarrassed and not at all amused, as though she had surprised Eppy nude and had had to watch while Eppy put on tawdry underclothes. Suddenly, while Nancy smiled politely, a tremendous throb of pity took her ... Eppy was acting, she was elaborating her romance exactly as Major MacArthur might extoll the glories of hypothetical Florida subdivisions, and on Nancy the effect was tragic; she became convinced that Eppy, for all her reading, understood the adventure ahead of her no more than she used to understand the words little boys chalked on fences.

"Eppy ... when are you getting married, honey?"

"Oh, we haven't decided yet! Jocelyn writes me every day. He wants it soon. But I don't know ... what do *you* think, Nancy?"

"June brides are the luckiest, Eppy."

"Oh, I'm sure he won't wait *that* long!" Eppy giggled. "You can't ever tell!" she trilled. "He's threatening to ride off with me like Young Lochinvar!"

Nancy's smile, if still kindly, contained honest mirth. She rose.

"Well, better not be in too big a hurry, old son. Make 'em moan and like it." She hesitated—good Lord! she wasn't Beatrice Fairfax! But she must say—"Tell you what, Eppy, we'll have lunch some time."

The spectacles beamed.

"Why, I'd just love to, Nancy! Where you living now?"

It struck Nancy, as suddenly as compassion had, that Eppy Spurlock was probably the one person in Corinth aware of Nancy MacArthur's existence who didn't know where she lived, what she did and most of the things Nancy MacArthur had done which she ought not to have done. Slowly she wrote on Eppy's pad.

"That's the address and 'phone number. By the way, I'm married myself, you know. ... Uh-huh. ... I'm Mrs. Antonio Bergo."

"Why—that's wonderful, Nancy! I'm so glad!"

"He's a right nice man, too, Eppy." She patted Eppy's arm. "You call me up."

"Oh, I will!...But I'll see you at Sister's won't I?"

Nancy cocked her head. "I had a date...but I think I can break it. Yes, I'm sure I can...I'll be there, Eppy!"

She cogitated, going down the library steps, exactly what had inspired that promise. Not curiosity about the old Lee Street crowd; it was something stronger—a pity and a fear bound around Eppy Spurlock—that would draw her into Howard Craycraft's home. Then, as she quickened her stride, thinking that she must not be late for Tony, she saw Howard Craycraft walking toward her in the sunlight, smiling, his hat off, and she stopped, angry because her throat had tightened.

CHAPTER THREE

EPPY RESUMED her Jean Cocteau after Nancy's departure, but she could not keep her mind on the pages. Either he repelled her or made her feel so stupid, and besides, she was too restless now to read; she put the book down and gave herself up to a glad-sad emotion that was almost light-headed.

Nancy had confused her dreadfully at first. Most women she could shame by mere frigidity when they entered the "restricted room." Even for men, with that shine in their eyes one tried to assure one's self was artless geniality, she could muster a squelch. But when the intruder was someone she had known in childhood, especially when she was Nancy MacArthur, whom Eppy had admired, envied and stood in awe of, she was apt to flounder into one of those twittery states her family always referred to as "poor Eppy's nerves." Such visitors, despite herself, she invariably expected to burst into laughter and to point at her ... "Why, Eppy Spurlock, what are *you* doing here?"

It had been a relief to receive Nancy's congratulations and to plunge into a fanfaronade of confession. Confusion had vanished as her mind caught fire from her own words.

No misgivings troubled Eppy that she had babbled effusively or been ridiculous or boring; no fear touched her that her ecstasies had differed in any way from the conventional flourishes of the usual engaged girl. She still glowed with self-approval and with joy in an audience that had been so attentive, so sympathetic and so unquestionably impressed. How nice that Nancy had looked her up! How sweet of Nancy to do it! And Nancy would be followed, of course, by others. As the news spread, they would come tumbling across the threshold... kissing her... telephoning....

Eppy swallowed rapidly. Her hands shook a little. She must, she decided, trim a hat to wear to Sister's party, and she would pick from the hoarding of stuffs in her closet a particularly becoming gown, one of those she had bought in New York.... And flowers... orchids would be best, orchids were New York flowers.... "Yes," she fancied herself saying, "Jocelyn sends them every day, isn't it terribly sweet of him?"... Her lips moved, gently forming the words. And, from thinking of Sister's party she began to think of the old friends who would be there, and from them to other parties long ago on Lee Street, when little girls in white dresses surrounded tables crowned with spun sugar, snappers revealing gay caps, and a cake with icing on it and candles winking softly....

Eppy was not an unhappy child. She sat in her grandmother's lap and heard her croon about a bonny blue ribbon until a sandman came and forty pixies out of a red fairy-book danced minuets on Grandmother's ear-rings. On rainy days the pixies were paper dolls pirouetting under a tin roof, and all one summer they were June-bugs tied to strings and zooming through a world of green and gold. Only the pixies inhabited that world, and Grandmother, and Mother, and the legs of a big booming man who smelled like over-ripe apples when he picked her up; later there was a squall and a red gnome upstairs.

Gradually, a neighborhood grew into Eppy's world, a typical American neighborhood of homes and big families and yards and vacant lots, and in winter attics and open fires. The pixies became children like herself. At their back doors the woods began, with picnics and rambles and the adventures of the changing seasons, and but yonder was the city—tall buildings, trolley cars, the stores and churches, schools and other neighborhoods and other children. They had the country and the town, they knew the soughing of the deep pines, the blare of parades. It was good to live in a neighborhood like that.

But something happened to Eppy's outlook on that world. It began, though she did not know it, the morning she went with Mother and Father to the strange place they called a Tabernacle. Then she felt nothing save wonder at the huge crowd, curiosity over the novelty of sawdust in a church, and both a yearning and a terror toward the man with a voice like trumpets. Luke, they named him, "Smiling Luke" Smith, and Eppy assumed that he was Saint Luke. He talked and talked; the crowd was very still and Eppy almost asleep, when music pulsated. Saint Luke began to sing—she was never to forget that song, "I surrender all, I surrender all, all I have I give to Jesus"—and suddenly her father was on his feet. He was crying, it was frightening to see him cry as children cry. He stumbled into the aisle... Mother explained that it was all right. Clutching her hand, Eppy listened and was comforted. "I am so happy, darling, so happy!"

Eppy was only five at the time of the tabernacle adventure, and she was "half past six" before she realized her world had changed. She could not sense the change merely because an old woman no longer sang of a bonny blue ribbon, whispering that such songs on Lord's day were wrong, or because a man no longer smelled of apples and began to boom of the Lord's will and the Lord's apostles. The apostles easily became the pixies of a new adventure, Sunday-School; the Lord himself was a pixie; and she was too absorbed just then with the unfolding neighborhood to understand that Satan, the relentless Adversary, crouched in Eppy Spurlock's world.

Knowledge, when it came, struck hard. The little boy next door had freckles and round, solemn eyes, and the chances were that his innocence was as complete as his curiosity when he suggested that to view one another in the nude would be a novel game. The Lord knew Eppy was innocent—and more obliging than curious—but the Lord hid Himself at the moment Eppy's father turned the corner of the carriage-house. Long afterward, when she could think of the episode without the shame they taught her, Eppy wondered if her companion in sin were punished, too. For him, no doubt, a wholesome spanking, and a precocious resolve to be more discreet when again at such interesting observations.

Looking back on her own punishment, Eppy was to conclude that there are inflictions worse than blows.

Spurlock did not spank his children, he prayed over them. Over their beds and their stricken, wide eyes he prayed, to an omnipotent and all-seeing ogre who hurled bolts in this life and fed cauldrons in the hereafter. He had one abomination, this god—or at least he did that night—and this abomination was impurity, a word Eppy was to confuse thereafter with quite another word, sex. "Blessed are the pure in heart," said this god, for only the pure shall see heaven.

So a brand was put, a scarlet letter on a child of six. For they whispered and groaned in the night about their first born (a child of six, Mother, does not sin the abominable sin unless it is in the blood) and Eppy heard their groanings and shuddered, because, of course, they were right, she was shameful, she was possessed, she must fight, fight the Adverary in her.

Nor did Spurlock, new-washed in righteousness, thrust all his burden on the Lord. Spurlock was vigilant and of others demanded vigilance. The weak must be shielded, the sinner saved from herself. When she started grammar school, Eppy's teachers must be warned that she was "nervous," a "queer" child, and report frequently her behavior. When at home, she must play with certain girls only, with boys at this time not at all, and her whereabouts must be always on record—"Eppy, what are you doing *now*?" Other children played "hiding" in the evenings after supper, but it was not for the suspect to run wantoning in the dark. She read, instead, carefully chosen books whose heroines,

as she grew older, made her tremble and blush when they permitted the sedate kiss of betrothal.

Spurlock was not an unkind man, merely a simple and credulous one. But the reformed drunkard became an extremist.

What Eppy thought or felt did not matter. Nervous indeed under their censorious eyes, she could have told them as she faltered into girlhood, how unnecessary their precautions were. In her spectacles, which too much reading fastened on her, and her odd clothes ordained as a moral strait-jacket, she could have assured them that she was altogether safe from approach save the derisive. She could have shown them in her heart neither rebellion nor temptation, only a dreadful wish for goodness and an ineradicable hurt.

Eppy said nothing. Mutely she obeyed, and mutely hugged her wound.

And so, at length, salvation. Spurlock's vigilance relaxed; fears slept, including Eppy's. She found a chum or two, girls whom her humble admiration flattered; she shone in scholarship; she was not without an unenvied distinction; she went to parties. But the reclamation had been thorough. At parties there were games and boys. Kissing games Eppy refused, sometimes with tears, to play. Others revealed her clumsy and bashful.... "Oh, the wife takes the child, the wife takes the child, hi-ho the carry-ho! the wife takes the child!" Once Howard Craycraft, who was the farmer's child, chose her for the dog. Next day she saw letters on the school fence, "E. S. is H. C.'s sweetheart." A voice jeered. Eppy ran home, and cried, and would not look at Howard for years, when some one else was H. C.'s sweetheart and she was the girl they asked Fred Prentiss to bring to parties because Fred was glad to come on any terms.... It was too late, then, for kissing games; Eppy was grown up.

Many things came too late. She was nineteen when Papa made his money. It was too late for college then; Eppy kept on with the library course and, being "nervous," never learned to drive the car. The others did. The boys did and Sara Lee. And Sara Lee went to Sweetbriar for a year. She had beaux and attended dances. For Spurlock's growth in grace had mellowed him. Though he never backslid into drink and continued to attend church regularly, his prospering years appeared to ease his spirit as well as his flesh and to give him things to think about more important than the Adversary. By the time Eppy was thirty and Sara Lee was demanding a roadster of her own, Spurlock had ceased to rail at cards and dancing, he had yielded to rouge, and even mention of cocktails drew from him but a feeble mutter. If, now and again, he turned a dubious blink on his elder daughter, he did it through habit and because he realized that she, who crept out of her books so seldom and then with an old-maid-ish chirp like a cuckoo's out of a clock, had become a stranger. Irritated, he kept up the tradition of "nerves"—it was a defense against his conscience. Eppy was watched as a patient rather than a sinner; actually, for all her family knew of her, she might have committed the follies of a Phryne undetected.

Eppy might have felt that freedom, at thirty, is freedom come too late. She did not feel so. Long ago she had won a form of freedom—within herself. And if her world lacked the tangible steel of motorcars, it lacked their gases, too; the creatures in her world were shimmering; their daring brooked no limits but her imagination's; she did not envy other folks their worlds. Only, sometimes, to possess a world is not enough; there comes a craving to display it, that other folk may envy you.

The hands of the clock silently made an obtuse angle from 12 to 5. As though a chime had struck, Eppy looked up and began to gather her books, and with these under her arm, she closed and locked the door and tip-tapped along the marble corridor.

Corinth smoldered with the last breath of Indian summer. Beyond the city, the golden-rod would be powdering the country roads, the sumac kindling the hills, and even here under the tall buildings the twilight held the magic of wood-smoke. Yet Eppy walked with no love of the land or its people in her heart.

She could remember, in the days when one went to the library for "Five Little Peppers and How They Grew," how the way home had seemed exciting and short as one skipped, careful to miss each crack familiar over two miles of sidewalk. Then the last mile was woods, grown suddenly terrorful until the lights of Lee Street glowed. Now she traversed a "white way" and the woods were rows of shops, she who had courtesied to friendly posts and stones could be startled by an excavation which surely was not there last week, Lee Street was lost among towers to the west, and her destination now was a strange house surrounded by strangers' houses.

Yet Eppy could be glad of strangers. Strangers kept the shops, strangers indifferently did one's bidding, strangers said, "Yes, miss, where do you want them sent?" and neither knew nor cared who the sender was.

In the new florist's shop on Black Street, Eppy ordered a dozen Marechal Neil roses and an orchid sprayed with lilies of the valley. They were to be delivered separately, please, on separate days, the roses to-morrow night, the orchid before noon Friday. Tortuously, she wrote two cards. She sealed them both and handed them to the clerk.

In the candy shop, the girl nodded and smiled.

"The same order, miss?"

"Yes, please, and the same address."

She had a note already written to accompany the candy.

In both shops she paid cash.

The telegraph office was Eppy's last stop. Here she dispatched a telegram. It was addressed to a New York shopping service and said simply: "Call me long distance Friday afternoon. Spurlock."

She watched the clerk count the words as though they were so many apples to be put into a bag.

"Seventy-eight cents," said the clerk.

He gave her change without raising his eyes, and she was glad that it is all in a clerk's day's work when the hands of strangers shake.

CHAPTER FOUR

"Y̲OU'RE LOOKING lovely," he had said, "lovely!"

"Yes? Thank you!" Nancy's surprise had been deliberate, and deliberately she had retorted, "You look fine yourself, Howard. But you are getting fat, aren't you?"

Howard Craycraft had laughed, throwing back his head in the old way she remembered.

"Dodging me with insults, Nancy? Won't work... I've been trying to get you on the 'phone for a week. Called you last night."

"Did you? I didn't know. Why didn't you leave your name?"

"Well... that big husband of yours... you never can tell."

"My friends are Tony's friends. He would have fixed you up."

"I didn't want booze."

"No? Sorry. We'd like your business."

His quizzical grin had been upsetting.

"Quit stalling, Nancy. When are we going to see each other? What do you say you meet me one afternoon next week?"

What he meant, she had understood as clearly as though he had used the words, "Will you give me an assignation?" She had wanted to slap him, at the least to march past him scornfully. She had considered the various things she could say.... "What do you mean? What are you talking about? Howard, that's all over; Howard Craycraft, you let me alone!"—and she had remarked slowly:

"Why, that would be nice. But I'm awfully busy these days. Tell you what, I'll be seeing you next Friday. I'll be at your house, at a party. It'll be nice to talk over old times with you and Sister."

Howard, red and huffy, had shut up, and she had gone on with a malicious wave, and Tony's arm afterward had been hard and comforting. But the chance meeting stayed like a bad taste in her throat—regret that it had happened at all, disgust that she must fence with Howard Craycraft instead of trampling him, and a dread that her flying colors had not altogether deceived. That was the worst, to know that Howard could make her heart beat faster even while she despised him. She despised herself for not mentioning the encounter to Tony.

2

Howard, sauntering on to the club, shed his annoyance immediately, for if Nancy had eluded his perception she had not dented his ego, which straightway assured him that, despite her stubbornness, it was impossible for this girl not to adore him. Canes were considered effeminate in Corinth, but if Howard had carried one, he would have spun it now.

Pleasantly he contemplated the prosecution of this adventure, which had been urging itself on his imagination ever since he dropped into the Bergos' with Fred Prentiss that night. Until then he had not seen Nancy in five years, and it had been more than ten since he thought about her.

What a conquest she had been! Pretty little tomboy, with those hot gray eyes and a torch of hair above her fierce young body. It was the war that swept them both away. He had been mad about Nancy, mad from the moment he took her, up to the very hour of his marriage to Sister. Nancy had wept in his arms the night before. "Why, darling? Why? Why?" And Howard, weeping, too, had not known what to answer—that curious and inexorable mandate in his gentleman's code that required virginity in the woman one married and could not forgive the lack of it though one's self alone were the thief. Something … damaged goods … "if she gave up to me, she'll give up to the next one" ... something cold and shrewd shut his lips and reënforced his will. He had gone nobly to the church next day, nobly resolved to keep his marriage vows to Sister. By the time he broke them, in France a few months later, he had managed to forget Nancy. But what a sweetheart while it lasted!

"As a general rule," he reflected, "it isn't safe to cross an old trail twice," smiling because that was a quotation from the book he and Bo had called their "bible" in college. Kipling. How did it go? ... "Things remind one of things and a cold wind gets up, and you feel said. ... " Well, he declined to feel sad over this particular memory. The woman was still bewitching, she had been his once, and he would make her his again, for there was a saying among the young men of Corinth that a girl will always come back to her first lover.

They were not, in common with young men everywhere, a company of complete cads. They attended to business eight hours a day, they worked patriotically for the welfare of their community and their class, they were kind to their wives and families, and publicly they respected old age, womanhood in the abstract, some other people's feelings, all society's laws and most of the state's. In appearance they were uniformly natty and in manner extremely winning. But they did not have much resource within themselves for amusement and even less without. Golf and the movies were about all the state permitted. That left drinking and its natural brother, venery, both condoned by society. So the young men, single and married, drank a great deal and went habitually after young women.

The young women, in the main, did not flee. On the contrary, being in worse case, since they lived in an age of electrolized household appliances among negroes glad to sweep and scrub for a few dollars a week, the women, having neither jobs nor, with some exceptions, golf to occupy them, drank harder and flirted more desperately than the men. Born too late for the practice of miladyship yet yoked to the gentle tradition, they were bored by a freedom that offered no substitute for building the American home. Their homes, they saw, got along excellently without them, and so did their children. A few malcontents skirmished with art, sports and politics, and paid the penalty of being regarded as eccentric. The majority took to bridge as the easiest way to kill an afternoon, bridge with highballs as a matter of course, and if the consequent impulses went no farther than to quarrel tipsily with their husbands, they were guiltless often for want of temptation. Many temptation discovered, and these not among a limited group, for the feminine leisure class included all levels and the railroad engineer's wife, who could afford her vacuum and her nigger as well as the vice-president's lady could, was just as bored, learned her "contract," drank her whiskey and as eagerly welcomed proxies for romance. Howard, appraising his chances with the bootlegger's pretty wife, was neither a rascal nor an optimist as amusements and opinions went among his contemporaries.

As he entered the City Club, where he was to meet Bo Chapman for lunch, Fred Prentiss hailed him before he could pass on.

"How 'bout a drink?" suggested Fred.

"All right—but let's wait for Bo."

He had avoided Fred instinctively, not because he disliked him—didn't he always stand up for Fred when somebody like Sister called him a bore and a bootlicker?—but because he liked Bo so much better. Big, deliberate Bo, with his perpetual innocence to tease and his good-natured loyalty to count on, forever stirring in Howard a paradox of admiration and derision, forever satisfying in him any doubts of his own excellence—"Old Bo's a prince, a real gentleman; only a few of us left, by God!"—Bo gave him something no woman ever had; with Bo he neither needed nor wanted other companionship. Fred was all right occasionally, but Fred was simply a minor habit one was too lazy to shake off. Fred talked too much. Always the same old boast or the same old grief, the food or the liquor or the hard luck he had just had, and always too insistent.... "That's nothing! Listen, you fellows, what happened to *me*!"—like a neglected cornetist in a band playing a sour note to get the leader's attention.

Fred said, "Christ, I got a hangover! What a night!"

Howard turned away impatiently.

"Let's look for Bo in the grill."

They walked across the lobby, Howard slightly ahead, Fred moaning of gallons and headaches and his inability to go to work at all to-day, and as they walked, men spoke to them, young men like themselves and older men whose rich garb and ruddy look attested their eminence. The latter were the chiefs and witch-doctors of Corinth, and the young men were the tyros and acolytes of the tribe, for the City Club, unlike the Corinth Athletic Club, where a lad might strut solely because he tossed a basketball well, raised the totem of business as well as society and welcomed to membership both the old bucks and the promising young braves of commerce. Fred had ridden in during the war on his Liberty Loan horse and some day, seizing his opportunities, would be a sachem; Howard belonged by social right and would never be anything but his father's son. Yet, of the men they met, nearly all hailed Howard and dropped Fred a nod; conversely, it was Howard who nodded back and Fred who greeted the greeters eagerly and by name.

Bo was not in the grill. They went downstairs to the barber shop, leaving word with the headwaiter.

"Where's Goober?" asked Howard.

Goober, a colored boy, got them a pint of corn whiskey. They began to drink it, with ginger ale and "setups," in a shuttered room next to the barber shop. All drinking in the City Club, except at the dances on the roof, was done in this shuttered room out of courtesy to the judges, state's attorneys and other public officials who belonged to the club. When the judges and attorneys drank, they drank in the shuttered room, too.

"Where were you last night?" Howard said.

"God, where wasn't I? Got started here with some fellows. Then we went out to the K A dance. Went from there to West Lake. By that time, I was stinko. Coming back, we stopped for another drink at Tony Bergo's. That's when I passed out."

"Tony Bergo wasn't at West Lake, was he?"

"Hell, no. We just stopped at his place for a drink. Not that I needed it. Boy, was I drunk! But like a damn fool, I kept pouring it in. That's the trouble with me, I never know when to stop. Give me three drinks and I'm all right. I can stop like that! Give me six and I'm just feeling good. But after that, good night! I'll keep right on pouring it in when I don't need it. That's what I did at Tony Bergo's. That's why I feel so rotten to-day."

Fred poured himself a second highball as though to prove a man's a man for a' that.

"Boy, do I need this one!" He drank slowly, put down his glass. "Tony Bergo's wife was at the house," he said.

Howard prickled with annoyance. He was used to Fred's laments, could submit to them regularly without even the emotion of weariness; what he experienced now was not impatience, rather, grudging interest and a bristling suspicion of Fred Prentiss's smile.

"Boy, is she hot!" said Fred. "One of the best looking babies around this town, let me tell you."

"What do you mean, hot?" demanded Howard truculently.

Fred smiled his sly smile.

"Oh, I don't mean anything—not a thing!" He sipped his drink, smacking. "I spent the night at Bergos'," he said.

Howard blurted, "If you're inferring you spent the night with Nancy Bergo, you're a damn liar!"

"I didn't say that."

"You as good as said it."

"Yeah? Well, I'd like to know if a man can't cut a little side-meat around this town without ... "

"What?" clipped Howard. "What did you say?"

Fred hesitated. He had suddenly remembered the gossip in Corinth about the time of the war. He glanced at Howard swiftly, abjectly.

"Aw—I didn't say anything. I didn't mean that—I said I bet she was hot stuff. But, shucks, I don't know anything about her."

"You're damn right you don't."

"Well … all right, then. No use getting sore about it." "I'm not sore. What makes you think I'm sore?" Howard drained his glass. "Look here, Fred, you ought not to pull that stuff. It won't do. You ought not to talk like that about girls in this town. Nancy MacArthur was a nice girl. What if she did marry this wop, Bergo? I don't hold it against her—if it did kind of cut her out of a lot of things. So far as I know, she's still a darn nice girl."

He looked steadily at Fred, and Fred returned the look, and they both knew that Fred was thinking Nancy Bergo is Howard's mistress, and Howard felt warm and pleasant again, hugging what Fred was thinking but telling himself how chivalrous he was to defend Nancy.

"Shucks," said Fred, "I didn't mean anything, Howard. I didn't know you felt that way about her," and he thought God damn him, calling me down like that, what right has he got to call me down like that? the damn snob!

They were amiably discussing hard times when Bo arrived.

3

At four o'clock, at the West Lake Country Club, Sally Chapman said to Sister Craycraft, "My Lord, they ought to be here by now! What time is it, Sister? It was just two when I 'phoned the club, and Bo said they'd be right out."

Sister laughed.

"You know Bo and Howard. When those two get together, no use to fret till they get their gabbin' done. … Consider yourself fortunate, Eloise, that you never married into the M-P fraternity, 'My pal!' "

"Oh, I do!" Eloise King shrugged. "I can't say any sort of marriage is very alluring nowadays. So stagnating, don't you think?"

"Well ... "

Sister stared at her legs, thin and straight in the sunshine where she extended them, rigid, above bright water. She didn't mind Eloise being catty; catty people just can't help it, she guessed. And probably Eloise was right about marriage, people seeing each other day in day out, getting cross, getting tired, wanting somebody else. ... She kicked her feet as if to kick away her thoughts.

"It's not a bad little mill-pond sometimes," she said mildly.

She might have been referring to the lake, which was little more than that in its rings of hills below the clubhouse. They had strolled down after lunch to watch Buddy—John Ashton Chapman, Third, to his public—embark in his "outboard," and the sun was so pleasant they had stayed. The lake made gentle gurgles, autumn had not yet dulled the fairways of the golf course and it was agreeable to sit on the little pier where Sally could keep an eye on the whitecaps kicked up by her son against the far shore.

"Aren't you afraid he'll fall out, Sally?"

"No chance. If he did, he'd just get wet. Buddy's a splendid swimmer."

Eloise King did not pursue the topic. Buddy, she had decided, was a very dumb child. Coming out in the car, she had sat next to him and tried to engage him in conversation. ... "When are you coming to New York, Buddy? I'll introduce you to a friend of mine who's a real aviator!" ... Buddy said, "He got a Lockheed Vega? Gilly Brandt's got a Lockheed Vega." ... Eloise was not sure. And who was Gilly Brandt? ... "Gee, don't you know?" Buddy, staring, evidently deemed her unworthy of enlightenment. But Eloise persisted. One of the most amusing places in New York was the zoo. Buddy would love it. The Aquarium was amusing, too. And the Museum of Natural History. She had been rather proud of her pæon on the zoo, which she said was in Central Park and full of the most amusing animals and snakes and things, had Buddy ever seen a giraffe? She was taken aback when Buddy turned large blue eyes upon her and inquired politely but firmly, "What kind a car you got in New York, Eloise? You got a Hispano-Suiza? Gilly Brandt's got a Hispano-Suiza." Eloise, confused, had confessed that she preferred taxis, and thereafter Buddy's interest in New York had plainly expired.

A very stupid child, a little barbarian of the Machine Age. But what else could you expect? They were all stupid in Corinth or they wouldn't stay there. That, Eloise decided, was the cause of a vague and irritating depression that had been growing on her.

It had been nice the night before to be welcomed so cheerily by the Chapmans, to be motored to a house surprisingly like one of those Westchester places and installed in a huge blue-and-white bedroom with her own bath next to it and a maid to unpack her things—to wake to bird noises instead of the crash of New York traffic, to sunshine thrusting through trees, to a tap on the door and hot coffee. Breakfast in bed had been nice after so many mornings of drugstore food gulped in a rush to keep a posing appointment.

"I love your place, Sally. Simply charming!"

"We like it. Of course, Corinth's not New York. I'm afraid we can't show you much excitement, Eloise. To-day I thought we'd lunch at the country club. Sister Craycraft's driving by for us. You remember Sister?"

"Of course! Such a sweet child!"

The sweet child had become a tall and beautiful young woman, this morning a young woman faintly haggard despite her smart tweeds, faintly taut under the happy-go-lucky air Eloise remembered. Sister confessed to a hangover.

"You and Howard party again last night?"

"No ... not exactly." Sister's loyalties demanded family fights be veiled. She smiled over her shoulder while she drove. "Sally don't approve my tipplin', Eloise. You'll have to keep me company at the club."

That, too, had been nice—the assurance that she had not fallen among Puritans. The cocktails Sister secured were real Bacardi.

Eloise had enjoyed luncheon. They talked old times, and she had been privately gratified to hear the fate of former playmates, most of them married, some dead, and practically none achieving a life beyond their provincial environment. They did not know artists, writers, actors; their world was as stuffy as Gopher Prairie. Only after luncheon was over and the "do-you-remember" theme worked out, did Eloise fidget.

Sally and Sister were discussing the local Junior League show.

"... and they had a director from New York, Raymond Bois. Maybe you know him—well, anyway, you've heard of him. Terribly good-looking! The girls were mad about him. He offered Joyce Rucker a job in the Follies and she would have gone like a shot if her father hadn't put his foot down. You ought to see Joyce, Eloise—wonderful dancer! Mr. Bois says she's better than Marilyn Miller."

Eloise had smiled. She was sorry, but Mr. Bois couldn't have anything to do with the Follies. Bobby Connolly, Gene Buck, Bernard Sobel—she knew all those people, and no Mr. Bois was among them.... Behind Eloise's smile were many hours of bootless waiting in the Ziegfeld anteroom.

On the train she had resented her fellow-passengers because they had seemed both stupid and arrogant, and she had clutched her *New Yorker* as a sort of ikon, a defense against their smug threat. Much the same feeling of the unappreciated outside began to nettle her again. Sally and Sister were not, perhaps, arrogant; they were trying to be quite nice in their way. But they were stupid, they were ignorant, they were like Buddy, interested only in their stupid little sandpile of Corinth, and they were so ridiculously complacent about it!

She told herself that she was glad she was an outsider, that she had "nothing in common" with women absorbed by babies and Junior Leagues and petty, small-town gossip. Thank heaven she had escaped such a cul-de-sac! And yet … and yet …

Something incredibly like envy was gnawing Eloise. These homes, these clubs, these motors and servants and days of leisure to shop and gossip and loaf in the sun. She tried to summon to her comfort a vision of New York, and could distinguish only the drip-pan of her room-and-alcove apartment. She estimated the cost of Sally's mink at a thousand dollars, and, flicking her last year's pony coat, found it insufficient to remember that she boasted friends who called Sinclair Lewis "Red," Suddenly, irrationally, Eloise demanded of the gods who watch over the intelligentsia what right these complacent Corinthians had to their clubs and cars, their maids and rich, Babbitty husbands she would not, of course, have off a Christmas tree?

Conversation languished on the pier. Eloise struck up. She hymned New York, fascinating, inimitable. The stage. The studios, artistic and cinematic. Gossip of the great. Anecdotes of the famous. She trotted them out casually, with little personal pats for each name, like a lady exhibiting her poodles at a bench show, and who among the hicks knew if they were borrowed from others' kennels? She dismissed a star or two with a shrug, blasted a couple of reputations and paraded some private lives. …

Her? But, my dear, I happen to know her leading man's been her lover for years. Her husband? Oh, he doesn't mind.

Eloise was enjoying herself once more. Sally and Sister had drawn closer, caught by the universal steel of scandal, and Eloise smiled patronizingly at their shocked faces.

"But, Eloise, how *can* he? I don't see how any man—"

"Why not? Civilized people don't mind these arrangements."

"Well, I guess I'm glad I'm not civilized then," declared Sally. "I know I couldn't stand it if I thought Bo was untrue to me."

"Nonsense, Sally! Do you think Bo has always been true to you? And if he has, that he always will be?"

"I'm sure I don't want to know if he ever hasn't. I don't want to think about it, even."

"There you are! It isn't the fact of infidelity, it's knowing about it. Isn't it more honest to face things intelligently and bravely? Bo's human—he might be attracted to some other woman."

"That's different—if he fell in love with her. I'd just die!—but I wouldn't want him if he wanted some other woman."

"Oh—you'd divorce him! What about the children? Wouldn't you all be much happier if you let Bo go ahead and have his fun and get it over with?"

Sister moved restlessly. She wished Eloise would hush up—would quit picking at Sally that way. She hated a picker, and she wanted, really, to like Eloise.

"Sally needn't worry about Bo," she said. "He's an old darling!"

"Well, you don't have to worry about Howard," said Sally loyally. "I'll bet you wouldn't like it, either, if Howard was untrue."

Sister looked at the lake where shadows gathered ... untrue ... no, it wasn't that, it wasn't even knowing about it, as Eloise said, it was the not knowing that hurt ... not knowing what he wanted, who he wanted ... knowing only that he didn't want you.

"I reckon I wouldn't," she said.

Eloise, who had been watching her, laughed.

"Well, if Howard's been faithful—! Don't tell me all the men in Corinth are saints or impotent. I'll bet Howard's cheated just a little bit, hasn't he, Sister?"

Sister knew, then, that she could not like Eloise, ever. She said: "Well, if he has, he didn't blab it all over the lot!"

Immediately she was sorry. But wasn't that what Eloise had been trying to say? Wasn't she saying all the time that she, Eloise, had affairs? Women, thought Sister, are funny. They huddle together and talk about sex like men do, only they're not square like men, they won't admit anything on themselves, they just hint and generalize and beat around the bush. And I'm glad, thought Sister, glad I said that; only I'm sorry, Eloise, I'm sorry!

"Come on!" Sister jumped up. "Let's go back to the clubhouse and get a drink, men or no men. What do you say?"

While they waited for Buddy, docking under protest, Eloise hummed a little tune. Once, fingering her hair, she said, "I'd like to see old Howard!" and Sister answered quickly, "He'll be tickled pink to see you, Eloise!"

But as they followed their long silhouettes up the hill, the words in her heart were, "He won't! Oh, he won't!" and they still beat fiercely there when Howard hailed them from the terrace.

4

Six grownups and one small boy. Two married couples and a pair of singletons. "This is Mr. Prentiss. Fred—Eloise! And you remember Howard?" Handshakes and glances, chatter and banter. Well, shall we have a drink? Well! Why not? Chairs, commands and chink of ice, all around a table. Sunset on the level lake, sunset through red liquor.... Daddy, ginger ale for me? Sure, boy, sure! This is a reunion, folks, looks like a party. Here's cheerio and *bon!...salute...skoal...prosit....*

It is relaxing, it is soothing on the glassed-in verandas of American country clubs in November.

They tarried at West Lake through a round or two. They rode in the twilight, singing old songs. ... Lord, do you remember that? back when we were kids! Adeline, sweet Adeline, put on your old gray bonnet. ... At home, with children sent to bed, grownups can be children. So married couples loosened up, and single folk let down....

It is intimate, it is liberating in American kitchens when the host mixes drinks and somebody tells the limerick about the young man from Rumania.

Dinner was at Sakko Inn because this was a party. Because the cook would kick at six, even our nigger. Because you fête a visitor and Sakko Inn is novel. Chinese and slightly wild, but excellent chop suey. Because—oh, hell! Let's go! Why not? But bring along some booze. They've got a good jazz orchestra ... "happy days are here again." ...

It is astonishing how alcohol can turn normal humdrum persons into voluptuaries, clowns, savages and half-wits.

But exactly why, near midnight, they were all piled in one car headed whizzbang into the country, when they could have gone back to her house or Sister's if anybody wanted another drink, Sally Chapman could not fathom. Nor did she try very hard. Sleepily she held onto Bo with one hand and onto the side of the car with the other. She was glad she had to sit in Bo's lap to make room. Fred Prentiss was sitting next to them with Sister on his other side, and in front were Howard and Eloise. Howard drove with one hand. It was maniacal driving. If they hit something, they would all be killed. Sally worried about that; and about the children, safe at home in their beds, please God; and she worried in a sleepy, puzzled way about everything, all this drinking, and whether she was hurting Bo's knees, and if Eloise was having a good time, and why Sister had been so mean to Howard tonight, dancing all the time with Fred Prentiss—Sister oughtn't to drink so much, I must talk to her about it—and after awhile Sally slumped her head on Bo's shoulder and stopped worrying. Thank goodness for Bo! He never got drunk. Bo was just there, and you held on.

CHAPTER FIVE

"GIMME FO' mo Scotch an' one rye," said Skeet, and plunked his tray on the kitchen table.

"Who say so?" said Mammy Pickett.

"Me, I say so."

"You! Who you? Say a hoot-owl say so, do jus' as well."

"Boss he say so. Mist' Tony say so. Fo' Scotch, one rye."

"How 'bout de money fo' de last drinks?"

"Ain' no money drinks. House drinks. Guest-folks drinks. S'ciety folks!"

Mammy Pickett grunted. But she got up from her chair and began to make the drinks.

"What you know 'bout s'ciety folks? Who in dar?"

"Big folks in dar. Mist' Bo Chapmans. Mist' Howard Craycraf'. Mist' Fred Pren'iss. All on 'em in dar."

"Who dey got wid 'em?"

Skeet shook his head. "Women-folks. S'ciety gals, I s'pec'. Ole frien's Miss Nancy. Call her 'honey.' Come-a-sashayin' up an' hug her an' carry on to beat de band. ... 'Oh, honey, we so glad to see you! Ain' see you in so long! Honey, is you comin' to my party? Honey, you sho' is lookin' grand!' "

Skeet sashayed up and down to suit the word.

"Mind yo'self, nigger," admonished Mammy Pickett.

Glancing at the door, Skeet scratched in his hair for a cigarette while Mammy Pickett continued to mutter over the drinks.

"Is dey drunk!" said Skeet. "Leas'ways, most on 'em. Mist' Bo Chapmans he ain' so drunk. Gimme a dollar. Mist' Fred Pren'iss he just kinda drunk, but not so drunk's he was las' night. Mist' Howard Craycraf' he powerful drunk an' havin' him a time!"

"What dey doin'?"

"Dancin' mostly. Hear de raddio? Mist' Howard Craycraf' dancin' wid Miss Nancy. Mist' Fred Pren'iss grab her fust but Mist' Howard bust in an' say dis his dance, Mist' Fred better had turn her loose. So Mist' Fred commence dancin' one de gals he brung. Yankee-talkin' gal. Mist' Bo Chapmans he ain' dance nobody 'cause his wife done gone to sleep right spang on top him."

"How many gals?"

"One mo'. Han'some, quick-steppin' gal. Call her 'Sister.' She de happies' in de bunch. Just a-laughin' an' cuttin' up! Say she want her a man, too, but Mist' Tony laugh an' say he gittin' too ole to dance, so she run out de room an' come back draggin' ole Major. 'I got de nices' man in de bunch!' she sing out, an' ole Major he sail right in two an' nothin'—hot t'molly!"

Skeet slapped his knee.

Mammy Pickett shoved the tray of drinks at him.

"Here, nigger—git a move on."

The swinging door opened to admit a gust of music and Major Wallace MacArthur. He was dabbing his face with a silk handkerchief.

"Lord, Lord! I'm afraid I'm out of practice for such goings-on.... What's that, Skeet?...Scotch?...Rye?...Get along with you!"

The Major sat down. The kitchen was pleasant, clean and bright and odorless save for the delectable aroma of spirits. He glanced behind him at the door, which muffled the music now, and then looked hard at Mammy Pickett.

"Mammy—?"

The old woman, puffing, mounted another chair and removed a box of oatmeal from a top shelf. A squat bottle behind it she lifted down, tilted over a small glass, recorked and replaced before she handed the glass to the Major.

"Ah-h-h- ... Nothing like Bourbon!" The small glass waved back and forth under the Major's nose. "Sit down, Mammy. You must be dead beat."

"Better had drink dat drink," advised Mammy Pickett. "Ain' no tellin' when she come in."

"Nonsense!" said the Major, "doctor's orders"—but he drank the drink.

Mammy Pickett seated herself opposite the Major. Her palms were spread on her knees. Resting, she watched him. He was staring at the oatmeal box, and he nibbled one end of his mustache.

"What's pesterin' you, Mist' Wallace?" said Mammy Pickett.

The Major signed. "Oh, it can't be helped, I suppose. You can't be a peaceful, law-breaking citizen without paying the price. But it's a damn shame she has to put up with this sort of thing, any Tom-Dick crashing in here at all hours of the night. D'you know, Mammy"—the Major might have been addressing a dowager—"the way young people drink nowadays it's a wonder they have any stomach left, let alone brains and morals?"

Mammy Pickett shook her head dolefully.

"All the fault of this damnable prohibition, of course," continued the Major. "It's making us a nation of sots and idiots. You take those lads in there. They're decent lads, young Chapman and young Craycraft. Good blood—I knew their fathers well. Why, old Governor Craycraft would shudder in his grave if he could see his son banging about like some tomfool in a two-dollar bawdy-house!"

"His papa was a han'some man," said Mammy Pickett. "A han'some man!"

"He was, indeed. And his wife was a handsome woman. The women these days," declared the Major irritably, "are no better than scantlings. All bone and gristle. You take that young woman from New York in there. I'll wager you," offered the Major, "she wouldn't fill a skillet."

"Law me, Mist' Wallace! Is she dat skinny?"

"She's worse than that," declared the Major, "she's got a skinny way about her." He glared at the oatmeal box. "It's this prohibition, Mammy. They drink and get fat, and then they starve themselves thin so they can drink and get fat again. All this reducin'—it does something to 'em, makes 'em thin and sharp inside. God save us from skinny women!"

Beyond the kitchen door, the music became louder. Male voices competed determinedly with the radio.

> "Weep no more, my la-dee!
> Oh, weep no more too-day—"

The Major snorted.

"When I used to sing that song, Mammy, it meant something. Ladies were ladies, and they had something to cry about, by Caesar! Now they don't weep about anything but the state of their hips."

Mammy Pickett watched him.

"Mist' Wallace, what's pesterin' you?"

The Major got up and walked towards the oatmeal box, and without a word Mammy Pickett got up, too, mounted the chair and served him.

"What's pesterin' you, Mist' Wallace?"

"Mammy, I don't like it—I don't like that young woman. She's skinny, she's Yankee and she's got a chip on her shoulder. I overheard her ... talking to what's-his-name ... Pennice ... Pennies ... egging him on. ..."

"What she want him to do?"

The Major poised his glass against the light.

"I wish," he said, "Tony wasn't here to-night. I think a lot of Tony. It'll be a damn shame if somebody flies off the handle ..."

"You see, Mammy," he broke off suddenly, "he doesn't know these people. They're Nancy's friends. Old friends. Old friends can play the very devil sometimes ..."

The Major gulped at his glass, but the opening door reassured him. It was only Tony, beaming.

He propped the door wide.

"Step into the bar, folks. ... Got a gentleman here right down your alley, Chief. Mr. Craycraft's an old Bourbon drinker. He's gotta have Bourbon or bust. Mammy, will you crack out some of that old Kentucky?"

"Yes, suh, Mist' Tony. ... Law, if it ain't Miz Craycraf'! How do you do, chile?"

"Bourbon," asserted Howard loudly, "is the only drink for gentlemen!"

"Oh, Howard—give us a rest!" Sister patted Mammy Pickett's shoulder and shook her finger at the Major. "You ran away!" she accused. "You ran away in the middle of our dance!"

"I did not, young lady. You deserted me for a handsomer man."

"Liar! ... Howard, make the Major a bow, honey."

"Bourbon," repeated Howard, "is the only drink for gentlemen."

"All right, big boy. ... Bourbon comin' up. ... Jeez 'n' Christ, Mammy, is that all the Bourbon ... "

"If you just reach me down from behin' 'at box."

They watched Tony lower the bottle, the Major gloomily, Sister with one eye on Howard, Howard leaning senatorially on the table.

"Best Bourbon only," instructed Howard, hiccoughing his corn. "Never drink anything else."

"Howard ... please!"

"You lemme 'lone," said Howard. "Drink Bourbon if I want to."

"He's okay, Mrs. Craycraft," said Tony. "Okay, ain't you, boy?"

"I know, but—"

"Come on, boy! Take this like Grant took Richmond!"

"General Grant, sir," said Howard, "was a Yankee bastard."

"I bet he was, boy."

"And you, sir, are a Yankee bastard if you don't think so."

"Howard!"

"Aw, he's okay, Mrs. Craycraft."

"You lemme 'lone," said Howard. "You lemme 'lone, old wife!"

Sister stood beside the Major. Little puckers formed around her eyes, little sneers on her lips. But she laughed.

"All right, old husband!"

The Major touched her arm—thin; thin as that Yankee girl's.

"Give him his head, child," he advised softly.

That, he gloomily thought, is the last drop . . . the last drop. . . .

Howard put down the glass untouched.

"Where's Nancy'?" he demanded.

"She's around, boy. Drink your drink. . . . Bottoms up!" As if he were rebuffing a stranger, Howard stared at his host.

"And what do you know about Nancy? The hell with you, Bergo—the hell with you!"

He stalked out with the measured dignity of the drunk who fancies he is neatly revenged, and for some moments there was silence in the kitchen save for the spurts of music through the swinging door.

"Oh!" said Sister. "Oh!"

Tony laughed.

"Don't mind him, Mrs. Craycraft. He's all right. . . . Come on. You and me'll see he don't walk off the porch and break his neck."

He took her arm.

The Major, left with Mammy Pickett, carefully blew his nose, inspected the result, refolded the handkerchief and snorted several times.

"There you are, Mammy. Prohibition! A young ass forgets his manners . . . his wife and his host . . . insulted . . . and a waste of good whiskey. . . ."

"It do beat all," said Mammy Pickett. She pushed the untouched drink across the table.

"It does, indeed," said the Major. He drank the drink.

"Where's Skeet?" he demanded.

Skeet came through the door.

"Skeet, where's your mistress?"

"She dancin'."

"With that drunken Craycraft?"

"Naw, suh, she dancin' Mist' Fred Pren'iss."

Skeet put his tray down. He did not look at Major MacArthur. He shuffled his feet while the Major studied him.

"What's wrong in there, Skeet?"

"Ain' nothin' wrong, suh. Not as I know of."

"Where is Craycraft?"

"Mist' Howard?—I don' rightly know, suh. Seem to me like he wid dat Yankee talkin' lady."

"Is Tony with them?"

"I don' know, suh—if he is or if he ain'."

The Major got up.

"I think," he said, "I'll take a stroll about. If any more of these Bourbon experts come in, Mammy—give 'em corn."

It was quiet again in the kitchen. Mammy Pickett sat with her hands spread. Skeet scratched in his hair for a cigarette.

After a while, "Uh, *uh!*" said Skeet, shaking his head.

Mammy Pickett eyed him suspiciously.

"What you uh-uhin' about, nigger?"

"It do beat all!"

"Whatall beat all?"

"Way dey carry on.... Mist' Bo Chapmans' wife she still 'sleep on him. But de yuthers—uh, *uh!*"

Mammy Pickett muttered.

"Dat Yankee-talkin' gal," said Skeet. "She make Mist' Fred git up and dance Miss Nancy. Look to me like she kinder sweet on Mist' Howard, way she grab him when he come out de kitchen."

Mammy Pickett still muttered.

"An' look like to me," said Skeet, "Mist' Howard he kinder sweet on Miss Nancy. He was mad!"

"Look like to me," said Mammy Pickett, "you better had shut yo' big mouth."

"Who?—Me?"

"You heard me.... What truck you got wid white folks' business?"

"Yas'm," said Skeet.

They did not talk. Skeet smoked a cigarette to the rim. Mammy Pickett looked at the clock. It was twenty minutes past one. At six she must start the range.

Somebody bashed into the kitchen door. A voice choked, "God damn you!" and a shuffle of sounds suddenly came clear like waves through static as the door sprang wide and Tony through it, dragging Howard.

"Get him in here, Chapman!"

"I'll kill him—I'll kill him!"

Howard Craycraft, panting and weeping, fought for release.

"Grab his other arm—grab his knife!"

Something fell, and Bo Chapman kicked it across the room.

"Good God, Howard—have you gone crazy?"

"I'll kill him! ... The sneaking little bastard."

Major MacArthur, closing the door behind him, said through the crack, "You keep out of this, young woman. You, too, Sister. We'll sober him up. And for the Lord's sake, don't let Nancy know." He stood with his back against the door. His eyes were small red marbles.

"What the devil is the meaning of this outrageous behavior?"

They were suddenly like abashed children, Mammy Pickett backed against the range, Skeet as close to the wall as he could get without climbing it, Tony and Bo holding their man. Howard hung limp between them. He had ceased to struggle.

Tony said, "Chief—I had to do it. He had a knife. They were dancing his way. Nancy and Prentiss. I—just grabbed him quick, sir."

"You're crazy, Howard—crazy!" said Bo Chapman.

"Turn me loose," said Howard sullenly.

The Major did not shift his red stare.

"What is the meaning of this, sir?"

"Turn me loose." They let Howard's arm go. He wiped one sleeve across his face.

"What do you mean, sir—drawing a knife in this house like a common thug?"

Howard shook himself as a dog shakes. He looked at the Major and sneered.

"Pull in your neck, Major MacArthur—you weren't so damn particular about your house or your daughter a few years…"

The sharp intake of breath was Tony's. All his muscles seemed to hump together.

"Tony!" cried the Major. "You keep out of this!"

He stepped between them and struck Howard in the mouth.

Howard blubbered, "Damn you—I won't take that!"

They rolled him back from the older man, Tony and Bo on either side, while he curbed and wrestled to be free. "Stop it, Howard! Stop it!" "That's enough from you, feller, you can't pull that stuff in here. Oh, good Christ!"

The door had swung again, erupting women, Nancy in the midst of them, blazing. Sister flung past her. She shook Howard and kissed him, shook him and kissed him again. Tears splashed both of them.

Nancy said, "Antonio!"

The large man let Howard go. He made a lumbering step as if to shield her from a repulsive sight, stammered, "Aw, baby—listen—" and remained beseeching her with his hands.

The Major regarded them. All of them. His daughter and his son-in-law, his daughter's servants and her old friends. All jumbled in the kitchen like Irish in a barroom … tears and whiskey … blows and kisses … Donnebrook free-for-all … the social scene, 1930. Mammy Pickett was handing the Craycraft child a wet towel, and Sister was sopping her husband's face while he pushed her away and sniveled against young Chapman. Skeet continued to crowd the wall. Near the door, what's-his-name, like a curious weasel, peered over the shoulder of the New York girl, whom the Major privately held responsible for everything. She appeared, in her skinny way, to be the only one getting enjoyment out of the mess, while the two persons he really wanted to spare anguish seemed about to start more explosions.

The Major removed his handkerchief from his knuckles and cleared his throat. If this were allowed to go on, Nancy and Tony were the ones who would be hurt. Once upon a time, when ladies' names were blackened, gentlemen lied like gentlemen.

"As a matter of fact, Nancy, it wasn't Tony's fault in the least. It was mine.—I—er—grossly insulted young Craycraft. I accused him of not appreciating Bourbon. I apologize!"

The Major bowed vaguely but airily.

They all looked at him. The Major stroked his mustache.

"All my fault. That damnable temper of mine. That and—I confess it, daughter—I'd had a few too many. More than the doctor prescribed."

His smile was a valiant attempt to be winning. It would be his luck, thought the Major, that she'd believe this last confession and no more. The battle-lights, he saw, were gathering in Nancy's eyes.

"My Lord!" drawled a sleepy voice beyond the door. "Where's everybody?"

They had forgotten Sally Chapman. She came in smiling through yawns.

"What y'all in the kitchen for? Drinkin' some more? My Lord, I hope to goodness I never see another drink as long as I live! … Bo, darling, please let's go home!"

"Right, Sally! What d'you say, folks? Come on, Howard. Sister, you bring him along. I'll drive the car. Well, Mr. Bergo, hope we haven't been too big a nuisance. Mighty nice to see you again, Nancy. You, too, Major."

They went in peace and jest, with good night cries floating back under the stars, and the Major, vanishing up the back stairs, thanked his gods for Sally Chapman. There, thought he, went a plump and proper woman.

But Tony Bergo, striving against that doubling of his fists that would give him away to Nancy, did not reach slumber so easily.

"All right, Little Innocence, they've gone, thank God! Now I want the truth!"

"Aw, listen, baby, ain't anything more to tell. They were drunk."

"Tony Bergo." He sweated pathetically under her level gaze. "I said the truth. What did that drunken fool do?"

"Your pop, honey? Jeez, Nancy—"

"Oh, Tony!" She stamped her foot. "Dad wasn't any more drunk than I was. Don't you think I can tell when he's lying through and through? I'm talking about Howard Craycraft."

Her anger distressed him more than her inquisition. Serenely he could have murdered Craycraft for inciting that. But it was too late now. The Chief—what a man!—had socked the right guy at the right time. Well, he could take a rap for the Chief.

"Listen, Nancy, no kiddin'. Your pop didn't want me to get in wrong with you and he did lie. Fact is, I was givin' a hot line to Mrs. Craycraft and her husband got sore. That's the real McCoy."

"Howard was jealous? And you were being the ladies' man!" Nancy regarded him beneath incredulous brows. "You men! All right, to-morrow I'll get the truth out of Mammy Pickett."

In the kitchen, Skeet wiped the last glass.

"Uh, *uh!*" he said, "we sho' was lucky we didn't all get 'rested! Ain' dat what you say?"

"Come breath or go breath, I ain' say nothin'—" said Mammy Pickett.

CHAPTER SIX

W HEN MAJOR MacArthur was a boy and knighthood, if not in flower, occasionally bore a late bud, the principal rendezvous for the hotspurs of Corinth was a saloon called the Oasis. There, one afternoon in the eighties, a certain Mr. Job Easley, given to boasting and being, it was testified, in liquor at the time, passed remarks concerning Miss Nina Fenton, a young woman of the town possessed of good looks but no social credentials. Her beauty had attracted swains who should have been knocking at nobler doors, and with one of these Mr. Easley was said to have laid a wager that he would escort Miss Nina to the picnic of the Woman's Christian Temperance Union. There was small evidence, despite the talk later, of Mr. Easley's insinuating more than his ability to squire the lady, or that Miss Nina was guilty of any indecorum save a pretty face. Whatever was spoken, however, got abroad, reaching at length the ears of a third cousin of Miss Nina's, one Thomas Fenton, whose righteous womenfolk demanded what steps he intended to stop the passing of the Fenton name in barrooms. Thomas had not seen his kin since the family rally for her father's funeral, but, with a vague memory of childish lips in his head and with his .32 in his pants, he hied him to the Oasis and there, after shipping a few, encountered Mr. Job Easley, charged him with a virgin's ruin, received the lie and shot Mr. Easley dead. The trial, and Fenton's quick acquittal, were a scarlet memory of Major MacArthur's youth. For matters did not end with a mere triumph for the sanctity of Southern womanhood. Incensed by the injection of their picnic into the scandal, the W.C.T.U. went on the warpath, smashed the Oasis, elected the defendant's lawyer governor on a bone-dry ticket, eventually secured state-wide prohibition and lived to rejoice in the Eighteenth Amendment, while the three principal actors in the drama achieved undying fame in the ballad which begins, "Come listen, now, good people, to Nina Fenton's fate" and which you may hear to this day, over almost any radio.

There was no good reason for Major MacArthur to brood on sagas of Southern chivalry on the morning after the drinking party in his daughter's home, for the party's direct consequences were what he expected, which was precisely nothing. Yet think of them he did as he overheard Nancy at the telephone. In the old days, mused the Major, it was thus; now, by the Almighty, you were a cad if you did not say to the dipsomaniac who had smashed your furniture, mauled your women and sullied your ancestry, "Forget it, old man, you were a trifle jingled!" Prohibition—bah!

Sally Chapman telephoned first. She said: "Nancy, honey, we were dogs to descend on you that way! You were an old peach and so was that nice husband of yours—and, Nancy, did you happen to see anything of my vanity? It's a little green enamel thing. ... "

Nancy said yes, the vanity was there, and she'd have Tony bring it by on his way to town; no, it wasn't a bit of trouble, and Sally mustn't feel badly about anything, "I was so glad to see you all."

Sister Craycraft telephoned at noon. She said: "We were awful, I know! ... Howard's 'specially sorry ... he says to tell you he doesn't remember a thing ... he doesn't, honest ... we both got hangovers ... how you feel, Nancy?"

Nancy said she felt fine, that of course she didn't have as much to drink as the rest of them, and Sister mustn't feel badly about anything, it was so nice to see them again.

"Well, you're terribly sweet about it," said Sister. "See you Friday?"

And Nancy said yes, she supposed she would see Sister Friday.

"Not that I want to go," she explained to Tony, "but I promised Eppy Spurlock I would and it's not her fault her friends married such little cutups. After all, we must put up with a lot—we're in the business!"

"Spurlock?" remarked the Major. "I knew a Spurlock who was the town drunkard forty years ago."

He was strongly tempted to sing them the ballad of Job Easley, but Nancy said, "You must have been pretty chagrined over that," and the Major decided to let well enough alone. He had forgotten that he was, technically, in disgrace. Borrowing a five-spot from Tony, he caught a trolley to the city.

Sally telephoned Sister. She said, What do you think, Sister? this silly Eloise King thinks you're mad at her about something, and Sister said, of course not, what makes her think that?... why don't you and Eloise come over and have a pickup? And Sally said they would.

Fred Prentiss called up the Craycrafts. Was Howard, he said, sore with him about something? He remembered there was some sort of fuss... boy, had he been plastered! And Sister said nonsense, don't be an ass... wait a minute... Howard says to come on out and have a drink. And Fred Prentiss said he would....

It was like that: as if alcohol had jumbled them into a grotesque dream in which their emotions fought naked, and now they agreed it was just a dream and they would laugh at it, recalling only those odd and humorous things they did, like the things in dreams one remembers and tells because they were crazy and funny. Do you remember, Howard, you wouldn't dance with me, you said I was General Sherman! Did I say that? Well, you said I was a saint, a Machine Age saint, you said I was Saint Hispano-Suiza.... But Fred was the funniest! My goodness, Fred, you remember when you thought the waiter at Sakko's insulted you....

It was like that. But it was also like this: as if the night had left with each one little secret deposits, little grudges to be tucked away into the subconscious, little newborn knowledges and interests to be let out only in swift glances and crafty, sidelong appraisals. They gave absolution in groups, and by twos they graciously condoned, but even in the group there were undertones and some by twos were franker—

2

Bo, sitting on the edge of Sally's bed at nine o'clock in the morning and handing her her second glass of water, said:

"Well, I've got to beat it. Listen, Sally. There's one thing I want you to do. Will you call up Nancy MacArthur and apologize?"

"What?" said Sally. "Oh, dear, my head! Where the children? What?"

"The children are all right. They're off to school long ago. I'm sorry about the head, hon. Listen, when you get up, will you be sure and call up Nancy?"

"What? All right. What for? What'll I tell her?"

"Tell her we're sorry. For the way we busted in on her and all the rest. You know—just apologize."

"Oh, all right. But I still don't know what for."

Bo creaked uneasily about the room.

"O-h-h-h," said Sally. "Where's Eloise? Is she up? Was Eloise all right?"

"She's all right." He stood by the bed, looking down, looking almost hatefully clean and shaven and robust. It was all very well for Bo to be a tower of strength in the darkness, but she did wish sometimes he drank and suffered for it like other husbands. She bet Howard was a sight for pity this morning.

"What's the matter now?" said Sally. Miserable though she was, she recognized his way of squinting at her when something was bothering him.

"Nothing," said Bo. "I was just thinking about Eloise. I was wondering—Sally, did she say how long she was staying?"

"Oh, dear, can't you think some other time? I don't know. A week. Two weeks. What earthly difference does it make? What on earth made you think of that *now*?"

"Nothing," said Bo, weakly. "I was just thinking."

He tiptoed along the hall past the door of Eloise's room where he had undressed her and put her to bed a few hours before. She had been pretty drunk, as drunk as Sally when he had undressed Sally and put her to bed, but still, that didn't account altogether for what she had said to him as he unlocked her arms from his neck, nor explain why she should have called him "Howard" when she said it. If any more wild parties were thrown during Eloise's visit, resolved Bo, somebody else was going to take care of Eloise, and it would be better for everybody's welfare, particularly Sister's, if Howard wasn't the caretaker.

Sally dozed desolately after Bo left; she would never, never drink again! When Eloise came in and got in bed with her, somehow their joined woes eased, cook brought them orange juice and coffee, and after a while they talked in more than plaintive cries.

"I don't understand it," said Eloise. "I never pass out—never! I think it must have been the corn liquor. How in the world you people stand it is beyond my comprehension. It's perfectly vile! I've been used to drinking such good stuff in New York, you know."

"Corn liquor's pure," quoted Sally. She shuddered. "I just can't stand the smell of it!"

"I always drink Scotch in New York," said Eloise. "Cocktails before dinner, of course. I like old-fashioneds. You should have one of Leo's old-fashioneds! And side-cars. I simply adore side-cars. But they're awfully potent. They're brandy and Cointreau, you know. Did you ever taste one?"

Sally wished Eloise would stop talking about drinking. "Who's Leo?"

"He's a bootlegger. I mean he isn't—he has a place in the Village. The cutest bar! You stand right up to it and have your drinks. But all the women in New York drink at the bars. They have some awfully smart bars, nothing like this dump we were in last night. Do you go out to the Bergos' much, Sally?"

Sally sat up. "I never went there before. But that isn't a bar!"

"Well, she's a bootlegger, isn't she?"

"Yes, I suppose so. Her husband is, anyway. He's one of the biggest bootleggers in Corinth."

"I should think you'd be afraid to go out there."

Sally laughed. "Oh, I know what you're thinkin'." All those New York and Chicago bootleggers carry machine-guns and kill you as soon as look at you, don't they? Tony Bergo's not like that. He's a right nice man. He was in the war and he owns lots of real estate. I bet he wouldn't hurt a flea."

Eloise admitted she liked him better than she did Nancy Bergo.

"I remember her," she said, "in school. She was rather pretty, then. The MacArthurs had money, too, didn't they? How in the world—"

Sally explained that they lost their money in Florida, and how it was something of a scandal when Nancy MacArthur married an Italian—and that sort of Italian, a nice man but, well, common—but Nancy always did exactly what she pleased, and it must be hard enough, said Sally, to be married to an Italian, and a bootlegger, too, without folks throwing it up to you all the time. "And she certainly was nice to us at her house last night!"

Eloise smiled.

"Why shouldn't she be? We drank enough of her liquor. It must have cost the boys plenty."

Sally guessed it did. She groaned. "Oh, dear, I must call her up! What'd we do to apologize for, Eloise?"

"We didn't do a thing," said Eloise.

"Well, Bo says we did. He told me to call her up and apologize."

"Bo's quaint, isn't he?" Eloise laughed. "So old-fashioned, apologizing to one's bootlegger! Really, I don't remember anything. Just before we went home there was some sort of argument in the kitchen. But that was the old man. He was drunk and began picking on Howard. It was merely amusing."

"Well, whether Bo's old-fashioned or not, I'll call her."

While Sally slowly began to get up, Eloise lay languid against the pillow, examining a finger-nail.

"She ought to know it wasn't Howard's fault," she said. "He was dancing with me and all of a sudden he left me—he was very drunk—I think we were laughing about Nancy and that Prentiss man, the way they were dancing, so—well, I'd hate to be her husband. Is she having an affair with Prentiss, Sally?"

Sally turned with one bare foot trailing.

"Who? Nancy? With Fred Prentiss? Good Lord, nobody would have an affair with him!"

"Not even Nancy? I suppose she was just ginny like the rest of us. Anyway, Howard said he was going to get another drink and … I remember now … a minute later there was a lot of noise in the kitchen and we all went out there. But it was just the old man. Why do they have him around? I suppose you can't help relatives on your neck, in Corinth."

Sally did not answer. She was picking up stockings from the floor and wishing Eloise wasn't so—so New Yorkey all the time. She understood, in a way, why Bo asked that question.

"I'll go call up Nancy, and I might as well call up Sister while I'm about it."

"She's sweet," said Eloise. "I wonder why she doesn't like me."

"But of course she likes you!"

"No. I don't think she does. She used to like me. It's funny. Maybe I said something last night. Maybe *I'm* the one who ought to apologize to somebody!"

She laughed at her own little joke.

"Silly!" said Sally. "I'm sure Sister likes you. She likes everybody."

She tossed her short curls.

"Eloise, will you look at my clothes! I must have been disgracefully tight. Oh, dear! I don't remember a thing! Did you put me to bed, Eloise? Was I awful?"

"You were perfectly tractable, dear," said Eloise, pushing back a cuticle.

3

The black girl who served the Craycraft household was not surprised, when she had let herself into Apartment 8-C with her latchkey, to find Mr. Craycraft's hat just across the threshold and his coat a few feet farther along the entry. Picking them up, she proceeded into the living-room where she observed a long huddle of blanket on the couch. That would be Mrs. Craycraft. The maid tiptoed past strewn female garments. She tried the bedroom door, softly. Locked. She listened until she heard snores. You never could tell, the folks you worked for these days, when you'd open a bedroom door on a throat cut from ear to ear.

Lavinia wouldn't have minded something like that. She had a friend, Maybelle, who was cooking for some white folks when a man up and died mighty quick. He was a big man, a rich man, the papers all wrote him up. But Lavinia didn't see anything in the papers about what Maybelle told her about the poison, and pretty soon after that Maybelle prospered and went away North. Lavinia was going away North, too, as soon as she could raise the money, and that wouldn't be long now, the way the Craycrafts left things lying around. One of Lavinia's grandmas had worked for a Craycraft forty years, supporting her entire family by pan-toting. Lavinia had little use for such archaic methods; she took a judicious five of the fifteen dollars in Mr. Craycraft's coat before she dusted it and went to the kitchen.

Howard had wakened at seven o'clock, gone to the adjacent bathroom for water and returned to bed. At nine, he waked again, drank more water and telephoned his office he wouldn't be down. At ten o'clock, unable to sleep, he put on his bathrobe and unlocked the bedroom door, puzzled because it was locked. In the living-room he found a cigarette and lit it.

"What are you doing in here?" he said to the huddle on the couch.

Her eyes opened.

"Sleeping."

Howard stared unpleasantly.

"You wouldn't let me sleep with you," said Sister.

She stated it without emphasis, as a simple fact.

"You locked me out," she said.

Howard spat a grain of tobacco off his lip.

"Did I?"

He seemed about to say something else, but after regarding her with the same sort of ugly defiance, shuffled out.

Sister lay with her eyes fixed on a picture, feeling the room silent and oppressive around her, feeling her clothes in a heap except for the slip she had on, feeling the couch hard in the nape of her neck and the pain in her temples and the inside of her mouth cleaving dry to itself, but not caring what she felt, not wanting ever to get up again, not wanting to disturb a muscle except to breathe, slow, effortlessly. If she got up, all the torpid pain would become active; if she got up, all the unhappiness that now was but a dull wash would rise in separate buffets, sharp and violent and demanding solutions.

The mere agony of a hangover, she didn't mind so much. You took bicarbonate of soda, you bathed and ate something, maybe you had a little drink, and after a while the headache and the torpor went away; like as not, you kept right on drinking, into good humor, into another bat. You were used to having hangovers; they were everybody's lot these days; among your friends, bromides for "the shakes" were as usual as smelling salts were in your mother's day. In the first years of Sister's marriage, hangovers were actually pleasant; there was something keener than passion in the comfort given and received by two who loved and suffered. Even later, when Howard first began to flare out at her when he got drunk, hangovers next day were the occasions of reconciliation, the sackcloth and tears and the sweet kisses of atonement. Now they were this stale murk in which she groped without the spirit either to denounce or reproach him.

I could do that, thought Sister, I could bring up all the injuries of last night and the many nights before it, the slights, the insults, the cruelty, and demand his apologies and beg his remorse. Why do you treat me like this? Why do you neglect me for other women? Be nice to them if you want to, but can't you be ordinarily decent to me? This King girl... I'm not jealous... but what if I am? She is so cheap, so transparent. Anybody could see with half an eye she was trying to make you. But you... you... you were such a fool yourself, drinking like a hog, running after Nancy, and Nancy didn't want you!... insulting me and everybody else.... Oh, Howard, I was so ashamed of you! And, on top of it all, locking me out of our room... "mine as much as yours." ... Howard, why did you do that? Why do you always do it? Howard, don't you love me any more?

Sister closed her eyes. She knew she would say none of these things. To humiliate herself by saying them, would accomplish only the added humiliation of his resentment—tit for tat, wound for wound, scar for scar, and already the scars were deep enough. They were like that story in the first reader—the boy drove the nails into the post, he drew them out, but the marks of the nails stayed.

Oh, I am not too proud, thought Sister, to battle or to weep. Not if battling would bring him back to me and make us like we were. But neither anger not tears seems to work any more. What is the matter with us? What is the matter with me? What can you do to recapture the vanished when there is nothing to tell you why it went away?

Across the dark pressure of her eyelids, phrases jigsawed from advice her mother had given her twelve years ago, after she and Howard had had their first quarrel. "Do not let yourself 'go,' dress well, be beautiful for him. . . . " In a city noted for its smart young women, Mrs. Craycraft stood out, and, if she were not beautiful, it was for no lack of facials, waves and lotions. . . . "Make his home attractive." . . . Well, wasn't theirs? Taste, money and care she had lavished on it; certainly it could compete with any other woman's in Corinth. . . . "Don't annoy him with petty household affairs, talk of the things HE is interested in." . . . Good God, if Howard would only open his mouth sometimes, she would willingly discuss anything! . . . "Don't sulk or nag." . . . All right, she wouldn't. . . . "Humor him." . . . She had made a profession of it. . . . "Try making him jealous, my dear." . . . She shuddered, remembering Fred Prentiss's wet mouth.

No use racking herself with such nonsense, no use. If the fault was hers, cause and cure were beyond her. If it was Howard's, she was equally baffled and hopeless. And perhaps it wasn't Howard's, maybe he couldn't help himself—people just can't help their feelings, or lack of feelings, can they?—maybe, decided Sister, it was just marriage; too much to expect of any two human beings that they can live together, day in day out, for thirteen years and not crack. But, if it was marriage, if it was merely a case of the affections worn away in the grind of the machine, like tubes burned out in a radio set, then what could you do about it? No matter how bright were yours, there were the other's, black, dead. . . . Dear God, what could you DO?

Well, you could get up and gather your clothes together and find some ice-water. You could take a dose of bicarb and drink a little coffee and eat a piece of toast. . . . You could say, "Golly, I've got a terrible hangover!"

"No worse than mine, I bet," said Howard.

Across the table where Lavinia had deposited the breakfast things, Sister studied him, the hair combed black and wet after his shower, the color quick in his cheeks. She marked, though, the red threads in his eyes, the swollen temple veins, his hand when he slopped the coffee.

"Poor boy," she said. "Why don't you take a little drink?"

Somewhere in Howard, a small door blew shut. Though it was small, it was an irritating door, opening on a corridor crowded with imps. They were his memories of every distasteful thing he had done last night—and of every distasteful thing done, or fancied done, to him. The first imps he had been thrusting back into the corridor ever since he got up, and the second he had been hauling out and grooming. These were ready to strut for him now; at any provocation, he was prepared to order a company of imps to his defense. But, suddenly, with Sister's words, he was glad to shut the door upon them all.

"I do feel rotten," said Howard. "I think I will have a pickup."

He rose and went to the buffet. "Thanks," said Sister. "Yes."

Neither spoke of the events of the night before, and when, after Sally 'phoned, Sister said she thought she would call up Nancy Bergo and apologize. Howard's opposition was feeble.

"I don't see why. They're used to drunks."

"Well, Sally did. She said Bo made her."

Howard mumbled something.

"Don't forget to blame it all on me," said an imp aloud.

For a moment, angry waves surged in Sister. "You were the one who insisted on going out there."

She wanted to say that, but she said, "You were all right.... I guess we all behaved like a pack of wild Indians."

He thought to retort, "Speak for yourself," but didn't. The imp stood consolingly beside him while Sister telephoned. You were all right, said the imp, you're damn right you were! There was some sort of row, but it wasn't your fault ... with Fred Prentiss ... you were dancing with that New York girl, or was it

Nancy?...say, Nancy was mighty sweet, but that New York girl was crazy about you...when all of a sudden they were holding you and somebody hit you in the mouth. Don't you remember? You were going after Fred Prentiss because...because...why, sure, because you didn't like the way he'd been acting with your wife. That was it...back there in the restaurant...and in the automobile...necking with her. By God, a man's not going to stand for any monkey business with his wife!

Howard settled down with the morning paper, feeling a good deal better, feeling pretty well satisfied with himself. He could even be magnanimous. When Sister answered the telephone's ring and said it was Fred Prentiss, Howard called: "Tell the old pain-in-the-neck to come out and have a drink!"

4

Nancy Bergo said to Mammy Pickett: "I want to know what happened in here last night. Come on now, Mammy—no foolishness!"

"Law, chile, ain' nothin' happen you don't know 'bout a'ready. Dey ain' do nothin'. If dey did, I disremembers. Dey was all right. Dey was drunk!"

Eloise King said to Howard Craycraft: "You must think I was pretty terrible last night—but in New York I'm really not used to drinking a lot."

"You were mighty sweet," said Howard. "Did I misbehave very badly?"

"Of course you didn't! You were terribly amusing."

"No—please!" said Sister Craycraft in the kitchen.

"You let me kiss you last night," said Fred Prentiss.

"Oh, that was last night...we were pickled."

"No, I don't want another," said Sally Chapman, in Sister's living-room. "Bo, darling, you've forgiven me, haven't you?"

"Be yourself—you got sleepy and just passed out."

In Ventner's speakeasy Major Wallace MacArthur was lifting one more last one.

"Did I ever tell you," he said to the customer at his left, "the story of Tom Fenton and Job Easley?"

"Only fourteen times," said the customer at his left.

"Don't mind him," said the bartender to the customer. "The Major has a little edge on tonight."

CHAPTER SEVEN

FRED PRENTISS had decided to play host. He had not hit upon this notion offhand, as some people do—"Say, folks, I think I'll give a party!"—but arrived at it after long thought and for a variety of reasons. And, once decided, Fred devoted still longer thought to the sort of host he would be, working out scrupulously the pattern of his party before he mentioned it to a soul. The party would be a tea. It would be Sunday afternoon in his apartment. And the guests would be limited to five.

Fred's plans matured on the third day of Eloise King's visit, which was the second day after they all went on the wild party at Tony Bergo's. Since the entertainment of visiting girls was a cardinal rule of the Corinth social order and since he had been the first Corinth young man to meet Eloise, he had been sensitive at once to his obligation and exceedingly bothered by it. For Fred did not like Eloise. She was pretentious and conceited, he felt, hiding her unimportance behind cocksure airs, and he was sure she disliked him as much as he did her. An evening with Eloise would be too much like tête-à-têting with his alter ego.

But a tea in Eloise's honor would do nicely. It would avoid the necessity of inviting her out, would actually be more impressive, would even take down Eloise a peg or two and show her that some of us in Corinth move gracefully in the New York manner.... "Mr. Frederick Prentiss entertained at tea yesterday at his home in the Beauclaire Arms for Miss Eloise King, of New York, the house-guest of Mrs. John Ashton Chapman." Yes, a tea was the appropriate gesture.

Furthermore, though the correct kind of tea would cost him more than flowers and show tickets, one tea would wipe out a number of social debts and put him better than even with the Chapmans and the Craycrafts. As he wrote down these guests' names, his slight glow of revenge increased, for teas were not common in Corinth; when the Chapmans or the Craycrafts formally entertained, they usually took a table for a dinner dance at one of the clubs. He would show them how the modern young man can be host both formally and intimately in his own rooms.

Fred thought of them as "my rooms" and he was proud of them. When he was a small boy, carted from boarding-house to boarding-house by a mother whose struggles and earnings and very bed he shared, he had acquired a hatred of dingy furnishings, cooking smells and community toilets that seared him with a greed for privacy. With his first week's salary as a runner for the bank, he had fled the seamstress's sign above a south side laundry, and now that he was a teller and baron of a suite in an apartment hotel, he cherished it as jealously as a mother-bird its nest. Fred never suggested a poker game at his place, the possibility of a cigarette on his Chinese rug appalled him. When some one dropped by, he was always fidgety until the caller left, frequently inventing pretexts to get rid of him, even if he himself had to accompany the intruder at the price of his own discomfort. The elevator boy had standing orders to announce these casuals before bringing them up. Mrs. Prentiss, who yearned to "straighten up the place," was permitted inside only to deliver his darned shirts and socks. Her offices, in point of fact, were superfluous; Fred kept the apartment as spick and span as a laboratory.

Yet he hankered sometimes, hugging his seclusion, for some one else to appreciate it...the curtains and draperies he had personally selected...the pieces of furniture with which he had augmented the hotel's...his books neatly arranged in their modernistic pyramid case...his cigarette boxes and lacquer ashtrays...his collection of blownglass figurines beneath the imitation Paisley shawl he had picked up in New York. The nude in water colors, which did not clash at all, in Fred's mind, with several framed photographs of movie stars of both sexes, autographed "Yours sincerely."

Against this background, he constructed a vision of his party, placing his guests here and there as autocratically as he placed the sandwich trays. The girls, arriving, would be ushered into the bedroom, where he must remember to have powder and rouge on the dresser. He would buy two kinds, the dark and the light. He made a note, too, of a small comb. The men could stick their hats and coats in the hall closet as they came in. The sandwiches and little cakes would be brought up ahead of time and placed in the ice-box in the serving pantry. There the liquor would be, no corn, but the real stuff. Or would it be smarter to have all the liquor on a table outside and mix the cocktails in front of the guests? He would ask Tony Bergo's advice about that, when Tony should come presently to deliver his order.

Let's see...if he put the ice and glasses and shaker on that end-table, Howard Craycraft probably would park on that side of the couch. Sally Chapman would be on the couch, since she always went to couches...and Bo Chapman would wait to sit down until he had gone over to the victrola and inspected the records.... "What? No hill-billy songs?"...Fred smiled. Bo would just have to suffer when, later on, Fred gave them his selected program. The Beethoven sonata and the Stravinski piece and "Scheherezade."...They would make Eloise King sit up or shut up. She would be across the room in the straight chair, he hoped, which would put Sister Craycraft in the deep chair, with the arms, near the window. He wanted her there, the light behind her head, so that when it got dark, when he played things like "Liebestraum" and "Tristan," her hair would be a nimbus and in the dusk he could drop casually onto the arm of her chair and let his hand fall on hers.

That little scene, of twilight thickening in his rooms, of the
slow curl of smoke from a cigarette, of the heartbeats of a vio-
lin drawing together him and the figure stretched indolent but
voluptuous in the shadows, was one Fred had imagined many
times yet never brought to fulfillment. Somehow the girls he con-
jured in the part, he had not the courage to introduce to it, and
the others, the sort who scarcely needed cadenzas to pipe them
to bed, he did not dare risk to the hotel gauntlet. Yet his dream
was no less sanguine for remaining evanescent. Sometimes he
saw the figure in the chair a slumbering tigress, lithe and black
of hair, sometimes she was blonde and cuddly, more than once
she was a well-known Hollywood enchantress, and there had
been moments when Fred hovered above a shape so undenomi-
nate that he shrank, frightened, from closer contemplation. Only
within the week had the figure taken on distinctly the attributes
of Mrs. Howard Craycraft.

He had known Sister years, he had danced with her in high
school days, he had read about her wedding with a ruffle of pride
in the acquaintance, he had encountered her fleetingly during
the war campaigns, and in recent years, since his intimacy with
Howard, he had come to think of her as a great friend. Or, rather,
of himself as the Craycraft's great friend. Never, until the other
night, had he looked on Sister with anything but what passed
in Fred for respect, a sort of servile eagerness to please her, the
society girl whom his mother might have sewed for once.

That Sister was not always happy, that she and Howard had
rows such as all married couples have, and that she must know
Howard "ran around," he had been aware without thinking much
about her. He had been a little sorry for Sister, perhaps a little
pleased, too. Most of his friends' griefs were a little pleasing to
Fred. Then, that night at Sakko Inn, the thing had come on him
like light at the end of a tunnel, a dim suspicion and suddenly a
glare—this girl was vulnerable, she could be "made"! He had heard
other men boast of similar phenomena. "D'jever just look at a girl,

Fred, and see it in their eyes? This dame, now, I'd known her God knows how long and never given her a tumble, and all of a sudden, she just looked at me and I said to myself, 'Brother, she's yours if you want her!' " ... but the experience had never happened to Fred exactly like that. He didn't know exactly what revealed Sister now ... her manner toward Howard, her insistent drinking, maybe her breasts suddenly lax against him while they danced? ... In any event there it was, the swift, wild possibility. In the car his arms had closed around her. Sister's head lurched. "Don't!" she muttered, and did not move as his mouth stopped her protest.

Of course, he might be all wrong, just kidding himself; as Sister had said yesterday, dashing him so easily, "We were pickled," and when girls were drunk, he knew by crafty experiment, they stood for stuff that really didn't mean a thing. But you never can tell.... "You never can tell, boy!" he had heard men say of those astonishing cases of intuition. And for that matter, the simple prospect of another necking party with Sister ... not Sunday, but on that later afternoon when, having once appreciated the quality of his place, she would return alone for a cocktail and music ... a necking party then, to the accompaniment of Schubert and twilight, was sufficient to send pale, anticipatory shocks through Fred.

His treason to Howard, far from deterring him, was not the least agreeable part of the business.... That damn snob! What a fast one to put over on Howard! ... on all that bunch ... with his bunk about nice girls ... with his holy air about Nancy Bergo.... That North Side crowd!

He began to think about Nancy Bergo, her red hair and her gray eyes with their black lashes, and the delicate odor of her skin, and to think about Nancy surrendering herself to Howard. The blood warmed in his throat. It was not inconceivable that Nancy, instead of Tony, would deliver his order. He saw her coming in the door, taking off her things, and the image in the deep chair became Nancy, languorous, unresisting. ...

The telephone rang and Fred jumped up, at once confronted by a realistic flash of Nancy's scorn.

"Hello," he said.

"Mr. Bergo calling, sir."

"Send him up," commanded Fred.

He was immensely relieved … I never get a break, he assured himself.

2

"Then you better get half a case of the Dunbar, too," said Tony Bergo. "If you got women comin', you want Scotch."

They had concluded the main transaction. The gin and vermouth glinted in neat array on the table, Tony filled the deep chair, and Fred, feeling quite the man about town as he faced his bottles and smoothed his dressing-gown across his ankles, had sketched the outline of his party for the bootlegger's approval.

"Don't think I'm tryin' to sell you somethin'," said Tony, picking his limp brief-case from the floor. "Case price on the Dunbar same as it is on other good stuff, but the Dunbar's imperial quarts and you get most a gallon more for your money, Fred. And, like I say, if you got women comin', you want Scotch."

"Oh, these are nice girls," said Fred.

"Sure." Tony offered a cigarette from a long silver case and took one himself. "But that's a funny thing. Know what I mean? You take women to-day and they ain't the way I always figured women. Why, I remember when I was a kid on the old West Side, it was plenty tough, but nice women wouldn't drink whiskey on a bet. Only the twists and the tramps. The Irish, they drunk beer, and Italian women drunk wine. My mother drunk wine and give it to all her kids. Many's the mornin', when she come home from work, she woke me up with a cup of wine for breakfast. Now all the women go for whiskey, the nice ones and the floozies both."

Fred smiled. Something simple and childlike about Tony; a good fellow for all he was a wop.

"What did your mother do, Tony?"

"Scrubbed floors. She had a coupla buildings on Broadway she started scrubbin' at six o'clock. When she got through them, she had a theater, and after that she scrubbed a cabaret at three in the mornin'. She scrubbed for old Cap Churchill once, which was how I got my first job. Helper in a bar. She was a swell woman, my old lady! She died while I was in the Army. Sometimes I think what a kick I'd get, huh? if she'd a lived and I could drag her into some swell dump like Churchill's and buy her the works, know what I mean?"

Fred nodded. He knew what Tony meant without comparing in the least his own pinch of filial devotion to a wop bootlegger's. Fred did not think about his mother, but about the Scotch. A case was entirely too much for his present bank balance, but maybe Tony was right, he really ought to have Scotch; if he got half a case, or only two or three bottles, at the case price—his lips moved in silent addition.

"How much is that Dunbar, Tony?"

"Eighty-four dollars."

"Well—look here—I'll give you a check for what I owe you, it's forty-six dollars and something, isn't it?—and instead of paying for the rest now, I'll take some Scotch, too, and we'll let the new bill ride for a few days—is that all right?"

The proposition was not unusual among the young men of Corinth. Ordinarily Tony would have said, "Okay." For he liked the young men of Corinth. He liked most men, the outlawed and the tamed, the tough and the respectable. He was inclined to lump all men together as good fellows until proven bad, and even then to shun a two-timer without bearing a grudge. The young men of Corinth were a finer breed than the young men of Hell's Kitchen; Tony recognized the fact and admired them no less for possessing something he had missed. Fred Prentiss, though not precisely his "kind of a guy," was one of the boys. To any detractor of Fred he would have protested, "Aw, he's a sweet guy," and in his mind he said that now.

He said it mentally to Nancy, whose parting instruction had been: "Don't you leave that little cheater a thing unless he pays for the whole business—and don't take a check!"

Nancy was too hard. He didn't mind her being hard on him, but when she was hard on him to make him be hard on somebody else, he winced. He could be hard, facing a hard man, but not when the man was a fellow like Fred, a little stingy, maybe, a touch of the violet, perhaps, but an all right guy.

"Of course," said Fred petulantly, "if you think I'm not good for it—"

He got up with a switch of skirts like the switch of an angry woman. And he was angry—angry that a bootlegger should hesitate to trust him, and panicky, too, remembering the bootlegger's father-in-law was in the bank to-day, talking to old Whipple, and what for?—but angry principally that he, Fred Prentiss, who had never had enough money, should have to haggle over money with anybody.

Tony said, "Aw, that ain't it, Fred!"

He knew Fred was good for it—why, a guy that worked in a bank would be afraid to have a check bounce back or let a bill go too long. He hated to play tricks on Nancy, but—

"Tell you what, Fred—you pay me now for this stuff and what you owe me and I'll bring you 'round three bottles of the Dunbar, enough for the party. We'll let the bill for the Scotch ride till you get the whole case, and that can be any old time."

Fred did a swift calculation.

"All right. To-morrow's Friday"—that check won't come through till next week—"can you deliver the three bottles some time to-morrow?"

"Okay," said Tony.

Standing up while Fred wrote the check, he still felt uneasy, as if he owed Fred an apology.

"You know how it is, Fred," he said. "Me, I don't care when you pay me, but Nancy keeps the books and she puts the bee on every dime. You know how women are!"

Chuckling, Tony accepted the check. He waved it back and forth to dry it, and Fred watched him. There was a malicious flicker far back in Fred's eyes and a nasty little whim formulating in Fred's head, where vanity smarted. Nancy, eh? So it was Nancy who evidently considered him a cheapskate and a bum.

"How is Nancy?" he inquired smoothly.

"She's swell. Listen, Fred, if you see her, you might better not mention the Scotch, see?"

"I won't." Fred snapped his check-book shut and tossed it on the table. As though in afterthought, he drawled, "You know, Tony, I like Nancy and I like you. It's none of my business, but you ought to warn Nancy to watch her step. Around town, you know."

Tony stared at him.

"What's the idea?"

"Oh, nothing particular. I just heard something. You know how people talk."

"What did you hear?"

"It wasn't anything to get on your ear about, Tony. Somebody said they saw Nancy and Howard Craycraft uptown the other day. Nothing to that, of course—they probably just bumped into each other—but the person who told me knew Nancy and Howard were engaged once, a long time ago—before the war, wasn't it? And—well, this person seemed to think it was sort of funny."

"What was funny?" said Tony slowly.

"Oh, nothing, really. But you know how Howard acted at your house the other night and—well, I hate anything like that to get started about my friends. You know? So I just thought I'd mention it."

Fred fidgeted. He wished Tony wouldn't stare at him like that. When Tony said, "Is that all you heard?" he answered eagerly, "Why—sure—that was all!"

"Well, forget it," said Tony, and pulled his hat to his brows.

He grasped his brief-case and walked to the door, where he turned and beamed.

"S'long, Fred!"

"Well—cheerio, Tony."

Fred locked the door. With his hand on the knob, he whispered, "You son-of-a-bitch," and then strolled across the room and let himself sink languidly into the deep chair.

3

Once, soon after they were married, the Antonio Bergos were in a New York night club when a waiter, hurriedly passing, dropped a note in Nancy's lap. She read it, laughed and handed it to Tony. The note said: "Shake that big palooka and have a drink with us, Red." Tony did not smile. He said "Excuse me," got up before she could stop him and approached a table where three men sat. They looked up, Tony said something, he stalked back to his own table, and a moment later the three men departed. Said Nancy, appalled but amused, "Tony, darling! You mustn't do things like that! But what on earth did you say?" He regarded her sheepishly. "Aw, I just told 'em to blow—what's wrong with that, baby?—when a guy starts somethin' with your woman, you finish it—see?"

That had been his philosophy then, and that was his nature and his impulse now—when a guy started something with his woman, though aggression limped on a flimsy crutch of rumor, the only way to settle matters was the direct way and the direct way was to challenge the aggressor and toss him out. But the big man driving his car away from Fred Prentiss' apartment was not the simple fellow who cowed a masher on Broadway; for the problem the big man grappled was not a simple problem of a cheap insult avenged, it was a muddle in which his own emotions were not the clearest. The big man was badly hurt.

For all that he was reared in the gutters of New York and banged about the world's back-alleys until he was nearing forty, Tony Bergo's conception of womanhood was approximately the same as it was when, at the age of twelve, he had fled a black-haired hoyden who boldly displayed him her curious anatomy. He had fled in shame, not for her, but for himself, feeling that in some way the sin was his and was perpetrated against all women, including his mother and the Blessed Virgin Herself. In time, he had learned not to flee, he had progressed from the doorways of Ninth Avenue to resorts not without international fame, yet never was he to lose entirely that sense of sacrilege, to satisfy the healthy animal in him without a struggle and without obeisance to the vessel that slaked his hunger, and toward the corruptest of these to exhibit a chivalry that, however crude or misplaced, answered his need of penance to the sex. For Tony, there were not two kinds of women, as with many men; there was one kind. She might be beautiful as the sun, and black as the pit, but she was still the Mother of God.

His very respect for womanhood liberalized his attitude toward women. Tony held no mandate for chastity. In a world where he had seen Justice sleep with the highest bidder, he had learned compassion for her weaker sisters. Most he had known were prostitutes, and among them workers of sturdy worth. Virtue, he suspected, was a poor horse to back, shy at the barrier, yellow in the stretch. No voice of tradition cried to him, "damaged goods!" for he had no traditions. When he met Nancy, he considered her, correctly, a woman without peer in his experience. When he asked her to marry him and she, looking steadily, said, "You know, I'm not what they call 'a nice girl,' Tony," he had answered, "Yeah? Well, I ain't no Nance—whatever we've done, that's all washed up."

He had meant it. When he met Howard Craycraft and Nancy said, "I had an affair with him once," he felt no shock of jealousy. That was "all washed up." By some innate process of generosity, he faced Howard's sin and forgave him for it. He could let Howard dance with his wife and insult him in his own house without too much resentment. A "no-good guy," but—the guy was drunk, he didn't know what he was doing, he was "a sweet guy." Tony himself would have considered castration before infidelity to Nancy, a choice simpler than would appear since she totally and permanently eclipsed all other women on his horizon, and to suspect Nancy of infidelity was to suspect his own sanity.

He did not suspect her, actually, now. What was going on in his head was more like a little ball bouncing in a roulette wheel. It would stop after a while in a snug groove labeled "hooey," but not immediately could he control it as it racketed among other grooves labeled Fred Prentiss, Howard Craycraft, Nancy and Tony Bergo. If it stopped at Fred or Howard things would be pretty simple—the direct approach, a few words and probably not even a sock in the puss to nail the lie. He rejected the impossible, that the ball could stop at Nancy. But it did linger an agonizing time around Tony Bergo, and Tony suffered—at the sacrilege of his misery, at the violation he did heaven in even hearing a slander against heaven's gift to earth. The sin, once more, was not another's, but his own.

He shrank from himself as he drove the Lincoln between the gates of his home, and though the sight of Nancy's Buick parked in the garage filled him with an odd relief, his very relief shamed him and made him curse the black heart that could harbor a fear of her being elsewhere with another man. He entered the house feeling as guilty as though he had seduced a nunnery.

Fortunately, since Tony's state of mind usually was like big print to his wife, he found her preoccupied. Or rather, so eager to describe her own afternoon that she had no inquiry for his. She had been shopping with Eppy Spurlock. Eppy had telephoned her, insisting that Nancy must meet her—right away—it was most important—and when Nancy had hustled into her clothes and dashed to town, the life-and-death matter had turned out to be—what? Eppy wanted help to make up her mind between two hats!

Tony showed his appreciation of this enormity by shaking his head and lighting his wife a cigarette.

"Of course," said Nancy, her indignation appeased, "that wasn't the whole business. She was buying her trousseau, and she had sense enough to know she knows nothing about clothes. She couldn't pick out a hairnet by herself. We looked at a million things, underwear, suits, dresses—apparently she doesn't own a thing—or maybe she has a hope-chest full—I swear I couldn't tell!—because she kept flying around from one thing to another, and most of them perfectly godawful, and chirping, 'Oh, isn't this lovely?' and 'Wouldn't a man simply adore me in this?' till after while I got dizzy, and by Jinks! in the long run she didn't buy a thing, not even one of the hats, because she said she had lots of time and she only wanted the hat to wear to Sister Craycraft's party to-morrow, and only half an hour before she'd told me she had to get all ready right away, that Jocelyn might send for her any minute!"

Nancy kicked both slippers off, swinging one stockinged foot across her knee.

"I'm dead beat. But I swear I couldn't be mad at her, she got such a terrible kick out of it. Why, you'd think she'd never gone shopping in her life! She had a potful of money, too, ready to pay cash for the whole works if she could ever make up her mind. She said some of it was her savings and some her father gave her for a wedding present. And finally she said Jocelyn sent her two thousand dollars. That girl's getting reckless as hell, you know, accepting money from a man and merely engaged to him. What's the younger generation coming to?

"Well," said Nancy, "I shouldn't laugh at her. Apparently she's mad about this man. Wanted to show me his picture, but then she went coy on me and said she'd left it at home but she'd bring it to the luncheon. Two to one she does and he's something pretty sad.

To hear her tell it, though, he's a cross between Rudy Vallee and Rockfeller, the reincarnation of a Southern gentleman of 1850, with a penthouse instead of a plantation and Japanese valets for slaves. That's all she can talk about, Jocelyn this and Jocelyn that, like a young girl with her first beau. Which of course is what she is. Poor Eppy!"

Tony took the swinging foot between both hands.

"I bet she appreciated you comin' along."

"Oh, that! She probably doesn't know anybody else to ask. You know what?" said Nancy. "I believe the only reason she did it was to give her a chance to talk. I don't believe she had to buy anything at all. As soon as she saw me, she started in on Jocelyn like a kid who's just seen Santa Claus. At first she began asking me questions, about the way men act when they're in love, and I was right embarrassed, trying to do you justice, darling, and still not brag about you. But, Lord, she was innocent enough, it was mostly stuff about presents and love-letters and the spoony sort of conversation you'd think went out with bicycles, and pretty soon I saw she was just pecking at me to give her a chance to trot out her romance and brag on *her* man. So I shut up and let her gallop. She'd look at me out of those horn-rimmed specs with her head cocked on one side like a canary bird's, and she'd blush and simper, and then she'd calmly come out with the damnedest mush you ever heard in your life, maybe something Jocelyn had written her, with the moon and the stars and a lot of poetry all mixed up in it, until you felt like you were reading something out of 'Saint Elmo.' You know, Tony, what I think? I believe Eppy's a little bit crazy! I don't think she's got any man at all!"

"She does sound kinda nuts," said Tony.

He still held Nancy's foot, and suddenly he bent and kissed her instep, and she drew lazy fingers through his hair, which was piebald black and gray and nicely rough, she mused, like Nipper the terrier's coat.

"Well, I'm awfully sorry for her for some reason," said Nancy. "And I'm kind of worried, too, I don't know why. It'll be interesting to see how she acts at Sister Craycraft's."

Tony got up and stood at the window, staring at the November dusk. Her room had been warm and sure around him, but out there it was dark and cold.

"You decided to go to the party, then?" he asked over his shoulder.

"Sure—I'll go. I've almost got to go. Why?—Don't you want me to go, Tony?"

His neck burned. . . . You heel, he thought . . . you dirty heel. . . .

"Sure, I do! Ain't I said all along you oughta go, you oughta see more your old friends? I want you to go!"

She regarded the neck.

"Well, don't worry. I won't bring that gang of drunks out here, if that's what you're thinking about. Is everything all right, honey? Did Prentiss pay you?"

"Uh, huh, he paid. . . . Listen, you're all in, Nancy. Let's me and you have a drink on the house."

He turned and kissed her, rubbing his chin on her smooth cheek, feeling her warm and sure. But, pouring from a Dunbar bottle, he thought about Fred Prentiss and he was miserable again, wishing he hadn't fooled Nancy about that Scotch.

CHAPTER EIGHT

THE DAY WAS perfect for a party. The sky was a scraped blue—it was like the sky in Italy must always look, thought Eppy—and the air was just sharp enough for the sun's pat to feel friendly on her coatsleeve. On days like this she could love Corinth if Corinth's romance only matched its weather. Standing on the library steps, waiting for Sara Lee in the car, she could almost imagine the street to be a glittering canal and herself a doge's daughter waiting to hail a dashing gondolier.

Eppy did not look like a doge's daughter; more like a nearsighted Cook's tourist, too plump to walk and to poor to ride, but perfectly content just to beam on the scenery. Her suit, though it was new and cost a hundred dollars, appeared bunchy as if from want of pressing, her hat was not smart, and the orchid she wore had not been pinned properly, it flopped as democratically as a daisy. Yet she did not feel badly dressed; she saw herself as she saw the day and the city, transfigured.

Sara Lee, not without heart for sixteen, conspired with the sun.

"You look swell, Eppy," she lied, and forbore to suggest that orchids are not the happiest flower for the tailored ensemble.

The sisters, with the gap of fifteen years between them, had never been intimate, but they "got along" in the fashion of a lively puppy and a tolerant housecat. Eppy enjoyed Sara Lee's company as she might occasionally enjoy a snappy modern novel, and Sara Lee humored and joshed "old Eps" with the indulgence of youth for kindly but doddering age. Now, as they sped out Cherokee

Avenue, Sara Lee chattered of the impending luncheon as if she were going to an exhibition of old-fashioned fancy work.

"I remember Mrs. Craycraft when I was just a baby," she said. "She and some other girls came around collecting for the war, or one of those things, and I thought she was divine looking. She use to wear Buster Brown collars and white spats, and she looked cute, but gosh! women dressed funny then. What do you s'pose she looks like now?"

"I guess Sister hasn't changed much," said Eppy. "She was younger than I was."

"Well, she must be thirty. She's been married ages, hasn't she? Her husband's awfully goodlooking, I've seen him at the dances, but he's an awful sucker for girls. I declare it's disgusting the way old men want to feel you up when you're dancing and try to drag you out to neck in a car."

"Do you neck, Sara Lee?"

"I neck but I don't pet"—while Eppy blinked, Sara Lee and the car rattled right on—"not unless the man's somebody I could go for in a really big way. Necking's blah. Gosh, Eppy, do you think Mrs. Craycraft'll have cocktails? I'd love a shot before lunch."

"You don't drink, do you, Sara Lee?"

"Only on third Tuesdays. Say, Eps, who's coming to this rumpus for you? I hope they're not a lot of static."

"I don't know," said Eppy, and her spectacles shone. "Nancy MacArthur's coming. She's a Mrs. Bergo now."

"Tony Bergo's wife? Now there's a woman," said Sara Lee. "I don't care what they say about her, she's the smartest looking woman in this town."

"She's sweet," agreed Eppy, and did not even wonder what they said about Mrs. Bergo.

The question of the personnel of Eppy Spurlock's party disturbed not alone Sara Lee. From the outset, it had puzzled the hostess. The notion of her old friends to greet the bride-to-be had been jolly, and the return of Eloise King fitted Sister Craycraft's plan. With Sally and herself, that made three who knew Eppy "when." But Sister had been hard put to it to select her other guests. Nancy Bergo was the fourth, and she had managed to get hold of Ernestine Hill, who wasn't in town often because she was a crack golfer and was forever tearing around the country to tournaments. For the life of her, Sister couldn't think of any one else. She knew dozens of women, but they didn't know Eppy. Sara Lee was a happy addition. She had forgotten Eppy had a little sister until she telephoned her for suggestions. But that had been Eppy's only one. In despair, Sister called up Mrs. Neal Carver, an older woman, but broadminded and a good mixer. Mrs. Carver was one of the best bridge players in Corinth, too, so that made enough for two tables.

A simple party, Sister had decided, was better than one of those bridge luncheons at the club, with forty or fifty women and so much gabble you couldn't hear the bid. Eppy would prefer a home luncheon, with drinks and talk and not even cards if they didn't want to play. But, at the last minute, Sister got panicky. She saw Eloise King's shrug and heard Eloise's affected voice, and she telephoned a caterer and a florist and a shop that sold favors, and despised herself for a coward. The favors were little dolls, so by way of reasserting her independence, Sister made up homely verses to go with each doll and dared Eloise King to sneer.

Eppy Spurlock's verse said "Here's to the bride! Happy shall she be! And may all her little troubles be as sweet as she!"

Nancy Bergo's said: "Of all the stuff I ever drank, there's none like our Nancy's, she is the darling of our hearts and as soaking wet as France is!"

Sister had debated that one. She didn't want to offend Nancy. But she was sure Nancy wouldn't mind.

Eloise King's verse took the most time. When she finally finished it, Sister giggled. It said:

There was a young girl from Manhattan
As pretty as peaches and satin.
She said to each male:
"Marry?—Don't be Airedale!"
And ended by takin' up tattin'.

If Eloise didn't like that, she could, by golly! lump it. The picture of Eloise and tatting was too wonderful to suppress. And the second line took the meanness out, felt Sister.

She perched the dolls cockily at each place around the table and inspected the result. Lavinia had set things very nicely, the center-bowl of chrysanthemums was a crash of gold and copper, and Sister gave herself a pat on the back.

"It does look jolly, doesn't it, Lavinia?" she said.

" 'Deed it do." Lavinia, in the starched maid's costume of which she was exceedingly vain, squinted judicially. "It look as good as any ho-tel."

Sister smiled. Through the high windows of her apartment, the sun poured a truce to sadness and the recrudescence of the world.

"Go 'long with you, Lavinia! It's got any hotel beat a mile."

She poked Lavinia in the stomach, and Lavinia giggled. When Mrs. Craycraft was in this mood, Lavinia almost preferred working for her to going up North.

"I feel gay to-day, Lavinia. Gay! Thank the Lord I haven't got a hangover. Is the stuff for cocktails ready? By golly, I think I'll have a little snifter before they get here."

Sally Chapman and Eloise were the first to arrive, with the Spurlocks and Ernestine Hill on their heels. There was a small cyclone of chatter around Eppy which Nancy Bergo's entrance increased. By the time Mrs. Neal Carver came in, the Craycraft living-room was like a busy phonograph store; the canary, happier than he'd been in weeks, led the hubbub.

Mrs. Carver paused on the threshold and put up a lorgnette.

"One, two, three—oh, damn! I never can see through this dingus!"—the lorgnette fell—"seven women! And all drinking like sailors! Where's the bride? My dear, do you wear panties or step-ins? I didn't know, so I brought both!"

Eppy crimsoned with pleasure.

"Drawers," she said simply.

2

Eloise King was curious—curious and a little disgruntled. You couldn't be really envious of this Spurlock girl, she was such a dumpy, dowdy, blinky creature, such a fool with her gush about her engagement, as if nobody else ever married a man before. But it seemed a crime if, as she kept saying, her fiancé was rich—and young—an athlete—Harvard—old family and all that. Imagine any sane man falling for Eppy!

"Who does Mr. Randolph work for in Wall Street?" she asked.

Eppy turned a flutter of eyelids.

"Oh, he doesn't work *for* anybody, he has his own business, his own concern, you know."

Eloise didn't believe it, but she murmured, "Indeed?" She herself knew nothing of Wall Street, but she'd ask somebody, she'd find out if they'd ever heard of Jocelyn Randolph.

"He lives on Long Island?"

"Yes...Oyster Bay."

"I know loads of people on Long Island," said Eloise. "Of course, the smart part's around the Hamptons. I simply adore Southampton!"

"Do you?" said Ernestine Hill. "I like the North Shore. Eppy, I wonder if I met your beau last Summer? Seems to me I remember a Randolph chap in that Westbury crowd. Does he play polo?"

"Oh, yes!" Eppy flushed like an eager child. "Oh, yes! I'm sure he plays polo. I wonder if you *did* meet him, Ernestine? He's tall and dark and—and distinguished looking. His hair's a little gray around the temples. I do wish I'd brought his picture!"

Eloise picked up her cards resentfully. There was that Hill woman chipping in her two bits again. The Hill woman seemed to have visited extensively in New York—she mentioned friends who were mere names in the society columns to Eloise—and, though Eloise didn't believe half she said, the Hill woman did rather cramp her style.

"Your bid, dear," she said to Ernestine, and wished she had gone to the polo game that Summer when Nicky had tickets from his friend on the *Tribune* but it was so hot they had just stayed on at "Leo's," drinking.

They were four, with Sally, at her table. At the other table, where they were playing contract instead of auction—Eppy didn't play contract—both the bridge and the conversation seemed livelier. Eloise wished she was over there, with that amusing Mrs. Carver and the little flapper, with Sister Craycraft, and Nancy Bergo, who was more fun than this bunch even if Eloise didn't like her.

What Eloise defined as liking people was really her capacity to impress or be impressed by them. She liked Sally because she could lord it over Sally, and, as soon as she heard Mrs. Carver was big-rich, she liked Mrs. Carver. She would have liked Eppy Spurlock if the humble and contemptible had not been momentarily lifted into the grand rôle. Eppy's little sister was impressionable, and likeable, but the other women—she thought of Nancy and Ernestine Hill—were blah. They seemed to regard New York as just another city, and who were they?—a bootlegger's wife and a girl who played golf and looked like a Lesbian. She had no means to awe them, and they offered nothing for her.

Sister Craycraft was more of a puzzle. She had put Sister down as sweet but dumb, just another of those mild wives who, like Sally Chapman, stupidly accept the good luck they don't deserve. Her advances to Howard Craycraft that night had not been so much to annoy Sister as they were the reactions of the born predacean toward the nearest and bestlooking male. Nancy had been her rival, Sister merely the wife. "I don't see why Sister doesn't like me," she had told Sally, and meant it, ready to be reassured. But the silly verse at luncheon had struck a sharp and unexpected warning.

"…and ended by taking up tatting."

So that was it. Venom was there—and a challenge. Eloise had laughed, too surprised to be angry, showing the verse to the others and declaring she meant it, Sister could have her old husband. When anger came, it was cold, the deliberate and malicious anger of a vengeful mind. She watched Sister, appraising her looks, calculating her strength, while a petty voice from their shared childhood whispered, "I'll fix you…I'll fix you."

"When's the wedding, honey?" said Sally to Eppy Spurlock. "You know, I must have a party for you, too. I'll give a shower. A regular, oldtime linen shower!"

These she-Babbitts, thought Eloise. With their showers and their bridge luncheons. It sounds too much like Social Circle, Georgia. Parties without men are no fun.

"But, my dear, didn't I tell you?" Eppy had put down the cards. "Oh, no, I guess I didn't, I guess you were out of the room. I was telling Ernestine and Eloise—may be married any day! I don't know myself. Jocelyn may have to go abroad suddenly. If he does, he'll wire—or telephone long distance—and have me come to New York and be married *there!* Isn't it exciting?

"Of course," said Eppy, blushes mottling her fat cheeks, "I'd like a big wedding, with a veil and bridesmaids and cunning little flower girls, but it's so much more romantic this way, don't you think? Maybe we'll be married in the Little Church Around the Corner, and go straight to the boat—maybe we'll go to Italy!"

"But, Eppy—how marvelous!—you mean he won't come to Corinth at all?"

Eppy nodded, round-eyed. "Uh-huh. Of course, I'd *love* for you all to meet him. But you will eventually!"

Eloise King thought: "You're not so dumb, my girl, to keep him away from that hot little sister of yours." Aloud she said: "If you go to Italy, Eppy, I'll give you letters. I have some very dear friends at Lake Como."

Ernestine Hill looked at Eppy, and Eppy, before she turned to Eloise, wondered if Ernestine had always had that twitch to her left eye.

"That'll be marvelous, Eloise!" she said.

But Eloise did not reply. She bent over her cards, for she had seen the wink.

Hatred shook her, hatred of them all, these patronizing, oh-my-dear females in their little puddle of swank and snobbery. These she-Babbitts, she repeated. The phrase was not sufficient. Bitches—thought Eloise—bitches!

3

"The last champagne I had," Mrs. Neal Carver was saying to Nancy, "was supposed to be Mumm's 1776 or something like that. It turned out to be hard cider and soap bubbles. But I'm a fool for wine; I reckon it's the sound of the pop; makes you feel so disgustingly elegant—you know?"

"Tony gets hold of some good champagne occasionally," said Nancy. "I'll have him watch out for some for you."

"Thanks. That'll be dandy! I should have met you a long time ago, Nancy. Tell you what, honey"—Mrs. Carver finessed the queen of clubs for a little slam—"if that husband of yours will bootleg me a couple of cases of A-1 fizz, I'll give you both a party, a real buster to christen the pool! I'm building an indoor pool for the Winter—you see?—though I can't swim a lick myself."

"Oh, please ask me!" cried Sara Lee.

"You're too young, child." Mrs. Carver flourished her lorgnette. "This is for old ducks only. Is that another highball you're drinking? Sister Craycraft, you ought to be ashamed of yourself!"

"Go 'long, Sister Carver! You're jealous because you're a teetotaler."

"I'll ask you, Sara Lee," said Nancy. "It sounds swell. But you do drink champagne, don't you, Mrs. Carver?"

"Nary a drop. I tell you it's the pop. I like to hear it. I like to see people enjoy themselves. You see," said Mrs. Carver, who had been born Cora Potts but never mentioned it, "I never did when I was young. People were too conventional. Girls didn't have a good time then, not even the naughty ones."

"Where were you raised, Mrs. Carver?" curiously asked Sara Lee.

"Child, don't ask me! I hate to think about it. In convents mostly. My folks were very strict. Old Puritan stock. They'd have kept a moccasin in the house before they would a cigarette. So now I smoke like old 97. Nancy, gimme a Camel! But drinkin's bad for my complexion."

Nancy obliged. She liked Mrs. Carver. She remembered during the war, when Mrs. Carver first came to Corinth from somewhere "up North," a widow of vague antecedents but commanding personality, there were people who said the rich Mrs. Potter was "common"; but after Mrs. Potter's marriage into the old Carver family, Nancy, who was in Florida then, used to hear of her Corinth triumphs, her generosity, the big parties at her showplace, The Pines, where envious gossips asserted the toothbrushes were solid gold, Mrs. Carver having acquired most of her millions from the well-known dentifrice, Aseptiline. Nancy fancied Mrs. Carver as the local duchess scandalizing the court and making them like it; she was, somehow, a symbol of redblooded rebellion.

Nancy was having a good time, and this was the more pleasing because she had not expected to have a good time at all. Her scorn of Corinth was too honest to harbor humiliation—when Corinth cooled toward her socially, that was Corinth's hard luck—but she had attended Sister's party warily, mainly because it seemed silly to stay away; she had come with a chip on her shoulder, prepared to hurt any one who tried to hurt her. Then, in the warmth of old friendships, in Eppy's ingenuous delight, in Sister's cordiality and Mrs. Carver's candid interest in the bootlegging business, resentment had vanished. It had been a long time since Nancy experienced so exclusively the society of her own sex. She was enjoying it. Even that showoff, Eloise King, wasn't so bad.

"It's a swell party," she said to Sister. "I like your Mrs. Carver. She's loads of fun."

"Isn't she? And I was so embarrassed, Nancy! Over those dolls. I'd clean forgot that old talk that Mrs. Carver made her money out of a nigger patent-medicine, and I gave her the pickaninny doll!"

"But she didn't mind. She liked it. Don't you remember? She said she used to be crazy about licorice when she was a kid and she wished she had a licorice 'nigger baby' now."

They were mixing drinks in the kitchen. Sister had let Lavinia go, somewhat to Lavinia's regret since the white ladies were beginning to get lively and Lavinia relished being around white ladies when they got lively. Maybe if that rich Miz Carver got lively, she'd give Lavinia a job in that big house where the bathtubs were solid gold.

"Well, I hope she didn't mind. I hope Eloise King didn't mind hers, either. It was sort of catty. You didn't mind yours, did you, Nancy?"

"Of course not. Damn good advertising. I wouldn't worry about Eloise. She probably had it coming to her."

"Don't you like her, either, Nancy? I thought maybe I was just a jealous little fool."

"Jealous of Eloise? Oh, you mean Howard." Nancy hesitated. She had forgotten Howard, forgotten Sister was married to Howard, forgotten in the pleasant Craycraft home that such a person as Howard Craycraft existed. "You don't have to be jealous of Howard," she said.

But Sister was pensive above the whiskey bottle. She nodded soberly. "I am, though. I can't help it. I used to be awfully jealous of you, Nancy."

"Well, you needn't be. I've got me a man of my own."

"Oh, I didn't mean that! I know you're crazy about Tony. I mean I used to be jealous before I married Howard. He was crazy about you, and you were so good-looking! I guess I'm a little bit drunk."

Sister giggled, and Nancy laughed.

"Why not? But you don't have to be scared of me, honey. If Howard starts anything with me, I'll send him home to his wife with a flea in his ear."

Sister was still standing there, staring at nothing, and Nancy perceived, suddenly, that her eyes were wet.

"Why, Sister—honey—"

"I can't help it," whispered Sister, "I love him so!"

Immediately she laughed.

"Excuse me, Nancy, I'm an awful little fool. First thing you know I'll be weeping into my beer like old women in Dickens. Gimme those glasses. I'll pour Eloise a rip-snorter. Too bad it's not arsenic!"

They dumped little cubes of ice from frosty trays. The whiskey gurgled, russet, gold, in bubbles of air. Here's for you. Here's for me. Here's for Sara Lee and Sally. Here's for Ernestine, with plain water. Eppy's still got hers. And here's for Eloise, dog-gone her! And Nancy, who had said to Howard Craycraft once, "I love you so!" and wept, told Howard Craycraft's wife to cheer up, no man alive was worth it. Poor kid! she thought, he is a rotter, he always was a rotter.

"Heigho!" said Sister. "I'm fine now. I feel too good for words! Are you having a good time, Nancy? I want *everybody* to have a good time!"

"I'm having a swell time!"

"Good. Then let's you and me push over a fast one before we go in. Here's how!"

"Happy days, kid," said Nancy.

4

The long distance call came at five o'clock.

For more than an hour, Eppy had been expecting it. One foot she had twined tightly around a leg of her chair, afraid she would jump when the 'phone rang, and over all her body cold prickles came and went. The others must have noticed how nervous she was if they hadn't long ago despaired of Eppy's bridge, if they hadn't been a little drunk. Eppy's own highball stood untouched, the ice melted.

Ernestine Hill, who drank little, did notice, but she put down Eppy's twittery symptoms to a natural state of mind. A girl as foolish over any man as Eppy indubitably was, you must expect to fumble the deal and go, off into trances and have to be told what was trumps. Ernestine felt protective—as she often did with feminine, soft women—whenever Eppy dropped her cards as if her hands were paralyzed. Maybe she was paralyzed. Ernestine recalled that Eppy had troubles as a child. Fits, or something.

"Oh, pipe down!" she rapped out, once, when the King girl made a little "tsk-tsk" against her teeth and offered to deal for Eppy.

The King girl glared and Ernestine said, heartily, "Sorry! I don't mean to be rude. But I can't endure that sound. I had an aunt who was always 'tsk-tsking' around the house and it's become a phobia with me. Sally, you remember Aunt Delia—"

By the time Aunt Delia's idiosyncrasies had been resurrected and damned, Eppy had finished her labors and the chance for Eloise to retort was lost. She sulked, cutting another notch in her score against the barbarians, and Ernestine congratulated herself on being one up at the turn.

She knew Eloise's kind. Greenwich Village. Home of the grudge girls. Bohemia their balm to futility. Dreary little tea-rooms and sordid little lusts. When Ernestine visited the Village, she despised and feared it, shrinking from those occasional women dressed like horrible caricatures of herself. What Ernestine liked was fresh air, a good brassie lie and a man to talk to who could shoot under ninety. Eloise was feminine enough, but she was unhealthily feminine, like a spoiled pet cat. Eppy was feminine—and unhealthy, too, perhaps—but she was a sick kitten and she was one of ours.

"Oh, I say, let's cut the bridge," she said. The hand had been particularly quarrelsome, with Eloise insistent on trivial conventions and Eppy, who played it as Ernestine's partner, going down four diamonds doubled. "Eppy's too much in love to be bothered and I don't blame her. Let's talk instead. You going to the football game to-morrow, Sally?"

It was then the telephone rang.

Eppy did not rise, but she jerked convulsively. The cold little prickles broke into cold sweat, for the ring was that long, imperative peal unmistakably long distance. She could not help crying out.

"Sister! If it's for me—"

They all looked at her, smiling, and Eppy blushed like a bonfire.

"I—I told them at home, you see—transfer the call—if—if it's New York—"

Sister danced in the doorway, waving her highball.

"New York calling! Oh, Love, Love! 's wonderful! 's marvelous! Eppy Spurlock, get on that telephone!"

Eloise said, looking up from the score, "We're ahead fifteen hundred points, Sally. At a quarter of a cent—"

But nobody was paying her any attention. She was, indeed, alone at the table, for they had all gotten up, shouting, laughing, and then suddenly hushed, waiting, flashing joyful glances at each other and at the closed door behind which went on an unintelligible murmur.

Well, this is one hell of a bridge party, thought Eloise.

The door opened. There stood Eppy. The moisture had settled on her spectacles so that they were two misty moons, and burst out in gobby trickles down her apple cheeks. She was trying to smile.

Oh, words, words! Where are you, words? The delicious little words chosen and rehearsed so carefully....

"Jocelyn says ... "

She swallowed, choked, the sounds she made were grotesquely funny.

"Girls—I'm going to be married!" cried Eppy, and burst into tears.

They closed around her like hens around the beleaguered chick, comforting, petting, wiping her eyes and bringing her brandy, asking questions, telling her to buck up. Eppy, you old silly! There, there, you're all right now, Eppy. For Pete's sake, Eps, anybody'd think you were going to be executed! And out of the tears and the gasps came calm at last and the news that Jocelyn Randolph was sailing for Italy next week and his betrothed, Miss Eppy Gordon Spurlock, must leave for New York City as soon as possible.

CHAPTER NINE

THEY WERE four now, Sister and Sally and Eloise, and Nancy, who hadn't meant to stay.

Amid excitement and confusion, Eppy and Sara Lee had departed to speed the bridal preparations, and Ernestine Hill had gone with Mrs. Carver.

"Why don't you come along?" said Mrs. Carver to Nancy in the bed-room. "I'd like you to see my place. We'll stop by a few minutes and then I'll drive you home."

Nancy hesitated.

"Come on, you won't have a good time here," said Mrs. Carver bluntly. "They don't, you know, after the boiling point. They'll keep on drinking because they haven't sense enough left to do anything else. You'll either have to get drunk, too, or be bored stiff."

"I know, I've seen plenty of it," said Nancy.

"That's the devil of prohibition," said Mrs. Carver, "your friends force you to drink. If you don't, they make you feel like a snob and a fool, and by the time you've sat around a while, listening to them, you come to the conclusion you are, and a dog to spy on 'em."

Nancy laughed. "Well, I'm not a snob and I'm far from tight. I'll come along."

But Sister had been so pleading. Gayly pleading.

Yet, when she looked at Nancy, flying that shadow of distress.

"Oh, please don't all of you dash just because Eppy had to go! The party's just beginning. Bo's coming by for Sally, and

Howard'll be home pretty soon. We'll have a real party! Nancy, don't you go!"

"But, honey—"

Sister caught her by the arm.

"Come here!—No, you come on here with me!"

They faced each other in the kitchen. Afterward, when the sting of outrage lessened, Nancy blamed herself for what followed. If Sister had been sober, distorted notions would not have obsessed her or would never have been spoken. Nancy knew Sister would not say, even unintentionally, a thing to hurt. But Sister was drunk and Nancy, though aware of it, could not control the uprush of anger that poisoned her and all the pleasant day.

"Nancy, you're not leaving because you're mad?"

"Mad? What on earth about?"

"What I said about you and Howard. Being jealous, you know."

"But, Sister, of course I'm not!"

"Well, are you mad at Howard? Don't go just because he's coming home!"

"Sister, you're funny! Why should I be mad at Howard?"

Sister stared stubbornly. "Oh, I know you won't say. But, Nancy, don't be mad at him! He was awful drunk at your house. He didn't know what he was saying."

"Oh, that," said Nancy. She stared at Sister, thinking back, at Howard's sloppy attempts to make love, at the scene in her kitchen, her father lying, Tony lying, Mammy Pickett unprecedentedly dumb. Suddenly she knew what they were hiding.

"You mean," she said, "what Howard said about me, that he'd—been my lover? Is that what you mean?"

Sister caught her arm again. "Oh, Nancy! I don't know what he said. Bo told Sally something, and Sally told me—please, I didn't mean to hurt your feelings! Truly!"

"I understand." Nancy pulled at her gloves. "Let's not talk about it. I'm not going on that account, if that's what you want me to say. I wouldn't have come, you know, if I'd thought—"

Sister began to cry.

"But you are going! And I don't blame you. Howard's a mess. We were having a good time. And now—now!—because he's coming home, s-p-p-oiling my pa-party—"

"Oh, bosh! If you think I'm afraid of Howard Craycraft, I'll stay!"

Nancy, furious, pulled off her hat. In the next room she could hear Mrs. Carver calling and the others chattering away, as they had all afternoon, only now their voices seemed to buzz lower and she imagined them talking of her; their heads together, whispering as Sally had whispered already to Sister; Ernestine's shrug; and Eloise's gloating smile—and Nancy hated them, hated Corinth, hated herself as bitterly as she hated Howard Craycraft. And she thought of Tony, whom she had submitted to the shame of hearing his wife slandered in his own home, and she all but hated Tony and her father for conspiring to spare her their knowledge.

"Nancy, please—please don't be mad!"

"Oh, I'm not mad! Just damn disgusted. It's not your fault, Sister. Here, make me a drink."

She went out and told Mrs. Carver she wasn't going yet, and a little later, when Sister brought more highballs, lifted her glass and to the world said defiantly, "Well—my health!"

Tony, returning home at six o'clock and receiving the message that Mrs. Bergo had telephoned she would be late, sat outside on the granite steps, watching headlights flare and die on the road to Corinth. The cold was dry and sharp in his nostrils, but he did not move until the white gateposts a hundred yards away were black. Inside, where fat pine blazed beyond the Major's head, Tony took a deck of cards to the window-seat and laid out twenty-five cards. Pick any twenty-five cards in a deck, and they will make five complete poker hands, provided you rearrange them persistently enough and refuse to let your mind wander to extraneous matters.

2

They were four, and had they been more, Bo Chapman assured them, he would decline to enter because, he said, four women of any kind were a handful, but four women all beautiful and all drunken were a handful and a half.

He straddled a chair, grinning at them over the back of it and feeling not at all dismayed or put out. Another husband might have glowered over this disconcerting climax to a hard day's work, but Bo was good-natured and Bo was married to Sally, who made most homecomings sweet but humdrum. He was rather entertained to find four girls stewed—and stewed, mind you, as the result of a lunch for a bride, one of those old-fashioned affairs we still associate with sewing circles. Well, well, what would our grandmas say!

"Sally, are you stewed?"

"Papa, darling! We've had such a good time."

"Eloise, are you stewed?"

"Really, I don't see what business—"

"Ouch! I take it back. Nancy, are you stewed?"

"Not if Eloise isn't. If Eloise isn't stewed, I'm cold sober."

"Well, I don't have to ask Sister if she's stewed. Sister, are you stewed, honey?"

Her answer was to sit on his lap and pull his hair over his eyes.

"Bo, we no more stewed than little rabbits. We just been toastin' Eppy Spurlock 'cause she married a count. She married him this afternoon over the long distance telephone and they're plane-sailing to Italy. I mean they're sail-planing to Italy. What'd

I say? Where'd you leave old mess Howard? Come on, honey, I'll get you a drink!"

Bo said no, he'd get his own drink, and Sister said no, he wouldn't do any such of a thing, and Sally said of course she was going to get Papa his drink, and Nancy said, the way they were, she'd better make the drinks herself, and they trooped with Bo into the kitchen so that, when Howard let himself in with his latchkey a few seconds later, he heard distant merriment but discovered in his living-room only one person, seated in the lamp's glow and looking at him with a vacuous smile on her face.

Eloise rose. Beyond a baffled irritation and desire to be spiteful to somebody, she had been feeling nothing until Howard stood on the threshold, and as she rose it is doubtful if she had any concrete thought except that a man had come into the room, they were alone, and she must make a good impression. She had read in books of women "swaying" towards men, and she had seen the feat accomplished on the stage. But Eloise was in no condition to sway. Howard protectively put out his arms and Eloise's plunge ended in them.

He held her gingerly, startled and a little embarrassed. This, he recognized, is Eloise King, and the others are making the noise in the kitchen. But, though he himself had had a few at the club and was keyed for adventure, he was not prepared to meet it staggering at him.

Howard looked down at Eloise's head, buried under his chin, and wondered what he should do. Eloise looked up, she smiled without stirring, he felt her hand move against his back, and he knew what to do. His kissed her. Eloise, too, who had been uncertain up to that point, knew what to do now, and she did it, thoroughly, for several minutes.

They broke, gasping, just before the others tumbled in.

"Hello there," they heard Howard stammer.

"Hello," said Eloise.

Howard and Eloise shook hands.

"Hi, you old son-of-a-gun!" said Bo Chapman. "Take a look at our wives, will you? They went and got fried on us. They said this was going to be a mild little party for a bride, but it looks to me like a wake. By cripes, it's getting so a man can't leave home for half a day without locking up the whiskey. It's not the iceman, it's the bootlegger that's breaking up families. Nancy, how about getting Tony to swap jobs?"

"I don't doubt he'd do it if you'll throw in Sally and the kids."

"Hi, Nancy," said Howard, "I didn't see you back there."

"Didn't you? Well, here I am!"

"Hallelujah! Let's—get—drunk!" cried Sister.

They all laughed.

In a flash, over the room where women had been gossiping, not quietly and something less than soberly, but intelligibly at least and with all surface signs of order and harmony, descended a sort of megalomania. It was as though, with the entrance of the men, who were merely the husbands of two of the women and no urgent cause for histrionics on the part of any of them, an invisible hand had sprayed laughing gas. Sister began to walk up and down, singing and flourishing her highball as though it were a drum-major's baton. Sally followed her, catching at the imperiled glass between shrieks of laughter, and Eloise became suddenly vivacious, snapping her fingers and stamping her heels in front of the radio, which she had turned on, it so happened, in the middle of Uncle Toby's Bedtime Story. Only Nancy failed to catch the fever of exhibitionism. She sat with her legs crossed, watching the others, and but for the curl of her lips, appeared unaffected by alcohol.

Howard turned to Bo.

"What are we going to do about 'em?"

"I don't know. What does the rule-book say about fried wives?"

"Pour it in 'em till they pass out. It won't be long now."

"How did our wives get so fried? Nancy's not drunk. Neither is Eloise."

"Isn't she?" said Howard sarcastically. "Boy, you don't know how you flatter me. Well, I'm several behind this gang. You've got a drink, haven't you?"

He crossed toward Nancy. To reach her, he had to pass Eloise, who tossed her head and over undulating shoulders, chanted "ha! cha! cha!—ha! cha! cha!" while she continued to stamp her feet and snap her fingers. She had switched the radio, which exuded thin dance music under a voice roaring the merits of condensed milk. Howard grinned and winked, but he kept on.

"What's new, Beautiful?"

Nancy refused to flinch from an old talisman.

"There's a football game to-morrow. Tech versus the University."

"You don't tell me! Want to go?"

"Thanks, we're going."

"May see you then. How about helping me tend bar, Beautiful?"

"You don't need help. And I'd rather you didn't call me that. I'm not exactly pining to talk to you, Howard."

"All right. Don't mind if I talk to you, do you? Come on out to the kitchen and let me talk while I catch a drink."

Nancy blew slow threads of cigarette smoke.

"Skittish?" inquired Howard. "I won't bite."

The others, Sister and Sally and Bo, were paying them no attention, and he had turned his back on Eloise, still vigorously performing her solitary ha-cha-cha.

He said, "I never knew you were a 'fraid-cat, Nancy."

She looked up, expressionless, at his quizzical smile and confident gaze.

"All right. I'll watch you catch a drink. Then I'm going home."

"I don't see what you want to rush away for." Howard, opening the door for her, was the genial, regretful host, and as they passed into comparative quiet, he continued his soliloquy while he roved around the kitchen. "This has the makings of a good party. We'll have some more drinks and then we'll all go to dinner somewhere. We'll go dancing or something. I'd like mighty well to waltz with you again, Nancy."

He put ice cubes and whiskey into a highball glass. Nancy silently handed him the siphon.

"Do you remember, Nancy, when we all used to go to Professor Monteleone's? Gee, I thought you were the prettiest little thing! You used to wear pale green dresses with big bows and a big green bow in your hair. I was crazy about you—but you didn't know it, I was too bashful. Remember the barn dance? And the hesitation waltz? And the Boston? Remember the time we were all in the Tissue Paper Ball and had to dress like flowers? I don't know what I was. Hope it wasn't a lily. What were you, Nancy? Sun-flower, wasn't it?"

She was leaning against the sink, and Howard, refilling an ice tray from the tap, considered her silence indicative of the sentimental mood.

"You know, we had a good time when we were kids. Seems to me you never have as much fun in life as you did then. Maybe the town's changed, maybe it's us—I don't know—anyway, the kick's gone out of it. Friends you have now, they're all right, but you don't click with them like you do with the friends you made when you were a kid. Don't you think so? I don't believe I've made a new friend, a real friend, in the last ten years. Even fellows in college. In the Army. I haven't any friends any more. There's Bo. There's—"

"There's Sister," said Nancy. "She's the best friend you have."

"Sure. I know. Sister's a great kid. But what I mean to say, Nancy, there never will be a thrill like the thrills you had then. Not for me, anyway. You remember my last year at the University? When you came down for the Thanksgiving dance?"

Nancy smoked silently. Howard, standing beside her, put down his drink.

"That's the first time I ever kissed you," he said in a low voice.

"Did the boys at the old frat house cheer?"

Howard turned red.

"What do you mean?"

"When you told them about it. You usually publish your conquests, don't you?"

She said it quietly, and his instinct was to laugh, a salute to persiflage. But he was too taken aback, too sensitive to the true target of her shot, to laugh. He got a little angry.

"Look here, Nancy, you've no call to say that."

"Haven't I? What do you consider sufficient call? You've informed my husband—shall I wait till you put it in the *Blade*? 'To whom it may concern, this is to certify that when she was seventeen, I seduced Mrs. Nancy Bergo, née Mac-Arthur'—in the name of Christ, exactly when does a Southern gentleman become a rotter? I suppose the answer is 'Never!' "

Howard's face was the color of brick.

"Who's been telling you all that stuff? Sister, I suppose. Well, it's a lot of God damn lies. I never—"

"Oh, shut up!" flared Nancy. "I'm getting out of here."

She flung past him, through the door. She was too exasperated to cry. Chiefly, she was exasperated with herself, for ever coming to the party, then for staying a single instant after Sister's revelation, and last, for permitting herself to lose her temper; giving Howard that much satisfaction, behaving like a tipsy shrew. She shuddered. But it wasn't my fault I was in this house, she argued; that was Tony's fault, he should never have let me come to this house, knowing what he did.

"I'm going home," she said to Sister. "No, you can't make me stay. I'm not mad, I'm fine. No—it's late—I've got to go!"

Violently they protested, Sister alternately marching around her and clinging to her, Bo urging her to dance, Eloise stamping over to ejaculate, "Ha cha! Don't go, Nancy. Ha cha! cha!" Even Howard, coming in from the kitchen and whirling into step with

Eloise, called out, "I don't know why she's going—make her stay, Bo!"

And Sally, upright but nodding on the couch, added her voice. If Nancy went, she was going, too. She was going home and look after her family. The others could do what they pleased; she wouldn't leave Nancy. And Nancy wouldn't leave her, either. Would you, Nancy?

"But I've got to go!"

Sally stood up, wavering.

"Aw right. I'm goin'. Nancy. Papa. Don't care wha' rest y'all do!"

For the first time Nancy felt drunk. They all seemed to be on top of her, hectoring, pleading, crushing, and she felt sick, too, choked with heat, smoke, noise and the radio's din. Her anger was stale bile in her throat. She tugged at her hat, sure that she must look drunk and despising herself for looking drunk.

"Got to go, got to go," she repeated stubbornly.

"Nancy—Nancy—please don't go!"

"If Nancy's goin'—I'm goin' Nancy!"

"Please—please—please don't go!"

"Ha cha cha! ha cha cha!"

When she stumbled, Bo grabbed her arm.

"All right … let's go. You, too, Mamma. Come on. Well, you said you were going with Nancy, didn't you? No, Sister, we ought to go, we really ought to. Come on, now, Mamma, come on. Eloise is staying, Mamma. Let her stay if she wants to! All right, Sister, we'll try to come back. Sure, I'll come back, maybe. … Come on, now, come on. Come on, Nancy. … "

The cold and the darkness struck them like the slap of surf, and while Bo drove with Sally's head on his chest, Nancy let the wind strike, let the darkness fold, let the wind and the darkness and the cold blow through her, until heat and reek and strife ebbed and she could close her eyes without the image on their lids of the suffocating room and the whirling couple and Sister saying good-by like a doomed man cheering.

3

When Mammy Pickett declared at eight o'clock that her biscuits wouldn't be fit to feed the hogs were they neglected an instant longer, the Major and Tony agreed that they should eat. The Major folded his newspaper, and Tony, with a last glance at the impassive night, followed his father-in-law to the table.

"She's probably dining at Craycrafts'," said the Major. "Skeet took the message and that nigger never got anything right in his life. Telephones scare him. Half the time he holds the receiver away out to here and just hollers, 'Yes, ma'am!' I've watched him."

Tony did not smile, but the Major, having seized the happy chance for a nip of Bourbon with his meal, was in rare fettle. He welcomed a silent companion, and Tony always made his best audience, anyway.

"I see by the *Blade*," he said, "that Cholly Semple has finally sold that shack of his on Stonewall Street and is planning to build a new house out this way. Something neat in mausoleums, I suppose. Jack Latimer must be doing well in the soap business."

"Latimer?" repeated Tony. "The big guy?"

"Um. Purity Products. Snowflake Soap. Kwiklean. Got more money'n a show-dog can jump over. Built the Latimer Building. Built the C. & Q. He's in Wall Street now and spends most of his time on his yacht. Jack's a local boy. Fine as they make 'em, too. Why, I knew Jack when he was just starting out. Nigger tenements—"

The Major chuckled.

"Say," he broke off, "did I ever tell you the story of Mrs. Jones Pelham's lawn party for William Jennings Bryan?"

"No, sir."

"Sorry, Tony. I forget sometimes you weren't raised with the village gossips. You didn't understand my reference to Jack Latimer and Cholly Semple, did you? Mrs. Semple's been Latimer's mistress for years, you see. Still is."

Instead of a smile or a leer, the Major's eyes held a faraway look.

"She was a lovely creature forty years ago. Nothing skinny about Sally Semple, body or soul. The Venus type. I'll wager there was no more beautiful woman in the whole South from the Potomac to the Gulf. Why she married Cholly Semple was just one of those mysteries. He was a dudefied, dumb sort of a ninny—still is—that's why everybody called him Cholly—and Sally was one of your gorgeous, opulent women. The men flocked to her like bees to honeysuckle. She could have had the pick of the swarm, too. But she married Cholly, and she stayed married to Cholly. And all these years, almost from the first, I'll wager, she's been Jack Latimer's girl."

"Why didn't she divorce him and marry Latimer, or something?" asked Tony.

"Son, decent people didn't get divorced in those days. You've no idea how uncommonly decent we were. It's true most of the gentry had a handsome yellow wench hid out 'yon side the hollow'—old General Blackstar died suddenly with his and there was the deuce of a kickup—but if I'd made love to your wife, or any white man's wife, and you'd caught me, you could have plugged me and walked out of jail like that! Nowadays, if a man makes love to your wife, you apologize for intruding and fetch him your dressing-gown. That's about the ticket, isn't it?"

The Major laughed, then coughed and furtively emptied his glass.

"I'm speaking impersonally, of course. The man who makes love to Nancy will wonder what hit him. Ahem! The fact remains that Sally Semple and Jack Latimer chose 'something,' as you put it. They had to, I guess. Lot of family pride involved. Elopement simply meant coventry as far as Corinth was concerned and they knew it. But I'll say this for them—they didn't knuckle under or apologize to anybody for having fallen in love, not even to Cholly. They were bold as bluejays. Nothing vulgar, of course, nothing indiscreet that people actually saw—public fornication was frowned on then—but Jack Latimer went everywhere with the Semples, they were a perpetual threesome, and everybody knew she was meeting him in New York, going off with him on the yacht and whatnot. Much they cared about gossip, though. They practically told Corinth to go to the devil, and that's what I like about 'em."

"But didn't Semple catch on?"

The Major shrugged.

"Search me. Husbands are the last to find out, they say. The poor fish may never have had the slightest suspicion. But I don't believe it. Semple wasn't a rich man and Latimer was, and it's a bald fact that Cholly owes all he's made in the world to Jack. However, let's be kind. Let's say Cholly's the typical blind husband. The world's full of 'em, no doubt. But"—here the Major decided from Tony's expression that he was really boring his son-in-law—"I'll get on with the story. From profane love to Bryan!

"You know Mrs. Jones Pelham. Beyond a doubt the vainest old tartar who ever wheezed. She'd snub the Holy Ghost if he wasn't kin to the Virginia Ghosts, but she'd crawl on hot coals to meet a syphilitic Frenchman with a handle to his name. Well, when Bryan came to Corinth—it was back in his crusading days, when all the women adored the silver-tongued knight from the West, 'the first crooner,' you might call him—nothing would satisfy Mrs. Jones Pelham but she must grab the lion.

"She gave him a lawn-party—'fiesta al fresco,' I think she named it—and everybody who was anybody in Corinth was invited. With two exceptions. Sally Semple and Jack Latimer. She didn't leave any room for doubt, either; she asked Cholly Semple—sent his invitation to his office and pointedly addressed it just *Mister*. It was about the time the Sally-Jack gossip was first getting around, and I suppose the old hag decided she'd teach 'em the wages of sin.

"Well, sir"—the Major leaned back and chortled—"that lawn party will go down in history as the damnedest ring-dang-do this town ever saw. Things began happening around ten o'clock. I don't know if Bryan was there, but everybody else was, the whole kit and boodle, dressed to kill, orchestras, refreshments, champagne in the pavilion, Chinese lanterns, all going to beat the band. And then she blew! First it was the police. A whole patrol-wagonful. They came charging along looking for murder and riot. 'Somebody' had 'phoned the station-house that Bryan was stabbed and the guests were lynching the assassin.

"Old Jones Pelham got shut of the cops without much trouble, but not without considerable excitement. The old lady was hopping mad. She called up the Chief himself. Gave him the devil. And about time she hung up, here came the firemen! They were a new bunch—we'd recently junked the volunteer system and imported some Yankee talent and equipment—and the boys were honing to make a show. They came clanging their horses and engines right up the drive, they dragged hoses and ladders across the lawn, and sure enough, one of the Chinese lanterns has to go up in smoke about then and some fool turns on the water and there's hell to pay. A lot of guests got wet and the lanterns were just about ruined.

"The firemen were still there and taking the bawling-out of their lives from the old lady, when three ambulances arrive. We had only three in town. The gongs made the devil of a racket. It was dark, too, on account the damage to the lanterns, and nobody knew if somebody had been hurt. But this is the prize rooster"— the Major cackled—"up the street and up the drive, without anybody noticing 'em much in the hullabaloo, trots a bony old nag hitched to a black wagon, and out steps, who d'you think? Hermann B. Schmidt, the cut-rate undertaker. He was diked out in his monkey-coat and a plug hat, and he was all swelled up with pride and joy over burying a Pelham, never having had a good corpse outside a Moose or a Red Man or one of those minor lodges, and he and his assistant were toting the cooling-board like they were all set to embalm then and there.

" 'Schmidt the undertaker—for the body, Madam,' he says to the first person he sees, who happens to be a guest and a woman. 'What body?' she screeches. 'Colonel Pelham's, Madam,' says Hermann in his best gates-ajar voice, and the lady swoons. Well, Hermann couldn't get it through his Dutch head that somebody was having a game with him, not even when Mrs. Pelham orders him off the premises. I reckon the old lady was too mad to talk plain, anyway—they say she cussed something shocking—and Jones Pelham had to prove he was alive by witnesses before Hermann would call off his embalmer."

The Major paused, suddenly aware that his auditor hadn't cracked a smile.

"The point is," he said, a little injured, "that nobody could prove a thing but nobody had a doubt who telephoned the police and the firemen and the undertaker. Mrs. Pelham never forgave Sally Semple for that night, but the next time she saw her—and you can bet plenty of people were there to testify—she spoke as sweet as you please, though I'll wager her face ached for a week afterward. And Sally smiled right back like the cat that stole the cream. Since then, most people have been speaking to Sally Semple, if they have to break their necks to do it."

"It's a funny story, don't you think?" demanded the Major after a suitable interval.

He waited.

"I say it's a funny story," he repeated.

"What? What did you say, Chief?"

The Major regarded his son-in-law with disgust. Probably five hundred times he had told that story with, until now, one hundred per cent success.

"I said," he said, "I think I'll have another whiskey. Skeet!"

When Skeet had come and gone, Tony said, "I'm sorry, sir. I'm afraid I wasn't listening. I was thinking about that Semple fellow. Seems to me he musta been wise to his wife and that other guy. Seems to me he couldn't help knowing, if he loved her. Maybe he did. Maybe he was wise. Maybe he was so nuts about her he just let it ride. Know what I mean? A guy might care for a woman so hard he woudn't do anything. If she wanted it that way—well, he'd take it on the chin. He'd want her to be happy—see?"

"I see," said the Major.

He twisted his glass slowly, inspecting the reflected light. The pouches of his eyes wrinkled.

"Tony—"

He checked himself. "Larrers catch meddlers" was a negro proverb the Major had heard all his life and, without clearly understanding, had nevertheless respected.

"What, sir?"

"Nothing.... I was just thinking—well, that you look a bit seedy. You're working too hard, Tony. Why don't you take it easy? Lose a little business, let some of these guzzlers go thirsty for a while, you don't need their money. As a matter of fact, you could quit to-morrow, couldn't you?"

"I'm in the black, if that's what you mean. But I gotta do something."

"Do something else then. Real estate—"

He stopped. Tony had risen. In the silence the approach of the automobile was unmistakable.

"Excuse me, sir—" The Major, alone, finished his drink with philosophic resignation. When God was not in His heaven, there would still be (one prayed) whiskey in His world.

Bo Chapman did not come in with Nancy. He walked with her up the front steps and shook Tony's hand.

"Hope you weren't worried, Mr. Bergo. It was all my fault we're so late. You're lucky at that; Nancy's comparatively dry; you ought to see the rest of 'em! We had to pour my wife to bed and the last time I saw Howard's she thought she was a locomotive or something. If they have any more of these afternoon quilting bees, I'm thinking of getting up a Society for the Protection of Absent Husbands—muzzles instead of chastity belts, you know."

They stood in darkness, and Tony groped for Nancy's hand.

"You better come in and have a drink, boy," he urged.

"Thanks, old man. Some other time. I've got to get back to keep the home fires burning. Besides, Nancy's seen enough of the Chapman family for one night. It was mighty sweet of you to help me, Nancy."

"It was sweet of you to bring me home, Bo."

"Not at all." He put on his hat. "Well, I won't keep you folks out in the cold. ... "

Silently they watched him go, the headlights of his car fading rapidly along the Corinth road, and in silence Tony kissed her—and kissed her again.

"Bo's a nice man," was all Nancy said.

But upstairs, facing her loosened hair and worn make-up in the dressing-table mirror, suddenly she let the floodgates fall.

"Oh, Tony! I'm sick of it, sick of it! Everybody—everything! I'd like to get out of this town and never see it again!"

Her head was up, her fists clenched, and he could only hover helplessly over her.

"They're lowdown, that's what they are, and I'm tired of them! I'm tired of looking at them—tired of hearing them, yaa-yaa and yaa-yaa—the women and the men—I'm tired of selling them liquor for their rotten parties, and putting up with them when they come out here—bragging and bluffing—bringing their dirty little whores with them—that's all they are!—getting drunk and sick and horrible all over my house—it's vile!"

She beat a fist on her lap.

"And they're no better in their own houses. We had to put Sally Chapman to bed, and she got sick, and the kids heard her, and the little girl—she's sweet and she's only five or six—she came in to see what was the matter with mamma, and before the nurse could get her out she saw it all and she just said, 'Has Mamma been making whoopee again, Papa?' and I think it's a damn shame kids have to be brought up in a country like this! Oh, I'm not going back on you, I'm not getting pure all of a sudden. It's a rotten law and we've made a fortune out of bootlegging and I'm damn glad we did, and I'm not taking any Holy Joe pose, either; I've been as bad as any of them, I reckon. But tonight I feel like pouring all the liquor in the house down the kitchen sink!"

Tony seated himself on the bed, letting her talk, letting her get it out of her.

"You think I'm drunk, don't you?" demanded Nancy. "Well, I'm not—I never was so sober in my life. And I had a good time for a while, too. It was fun seeing the girls and playing decent bridge, and I like that Mrs. Neal Carver—you know who she is, she was there and I think she liked me—and poor Eppy Spurlock was too sweet and pathetic for words—but they went home and things got messy after the men came—and something happened—oh, Tony, I'm furious with you! Furious! How could you let me go to the Craycrafts' after what happened the other night?"

His dark, sudden flush increased her exasperation.

"Don't you dare pretend any more! You lied to me—oh, I knew you did!—but you knew I didn't know all that happened! It was shameful not to tell me—to let me go to that man's house after he'd talked that way about me—and in front of you—"

A sob retched her like a bludgeon descending brutally and inexorably before his eyes, and Tony got up. She had put her head in her arms and she did not sense that he had moved until she heard him at the bureau, jerking and rummaging.

"Tony! What are you doing?"

He drove a drawer shut and opened another.

"Tony! Answer me!"

Obediently he about-faced.

"It ain't here. The hell with it!"

"Tony!"

"Listen, baby, you rest up. Eat some'n. Make your pop fix you a drink."

"Where do you think you're going?" she said quietly. "If you're going out to shoot Howard, that'll help a lot. I can't think of anything I'd like better right now than a murder scandal in this family. And if you're going out to beat up Howard, you should have done that two nights ago."

"I woulda—if your pop hadn't socked him first!"

He blurted like a cornered bad boy, stung to retort, and Nancy, after a long stare of amazement, laughed.

"So that was it. Well, good for pop!—he always claimed he had fightin' blood in him. But it's not going to do any good to sock Howard again. He hasn't done anything to you, Tony."

"He ain't. How about my wife?"

"He hasn't done anything to me."

"Well, how about this afternoon? You said—"

"I said nothing of the sort. Something happened—but that wasn't Howard's fault. Howard behaved like a gentleman today. Before he came in one of the girls spoke out of turn—that was all. She didn't mean any harm. And I'm not going to have you start socking women, Tony."

She knew while she said it that he would believe her did she declare the entire male sex stainless, and she suffered a pang for her mild deception. He was so palpably miserable standing there, so desperately in need to cure his misery with combat. Almost she wished she had let him go and wreak on Howard his deserts. What she could not know was the true cause of Tony's anguish, or that her words were caustic to it.

His eyes had not left hers.

"Nancy—baby—" he said, and choked.

"Well?"

She was cool now, having won a victory.

"You—like this guy? Do you love him, Nancy?"

She had been prepared for questions, but not for this. She had expected his anxiety and not undeliberately provoked his wrath, and in them her own hurt was healed. To storm a little, to weep a little, to lie a little—these assuage the heart and open it to peace. And peace she was waiting for, when he said what he said.

"What?" she whispered. "What did you say?"

His back was against the door, his arms wrenched behind him, and because he was tall and must look down at her, his head seemed bowed like a culprit's. She could feel his eyes yearning out from under at her, like the eyes of Nipper, the fox terrier, when she was eating candy and Nipper would stand with head drooped and only the wistful eyes lifted, and suddenly she could bear Tony's eyes no longer.

"Oh!" she cried. "Oh!" and put her hands to her face.

Tony left the door. He knelt beside her, tugging at the pressed hands, kissing them, forcing them against his mouth, striking them against his forehead as though to punish himself, and saying over and over, "Don't, baby, don't, don't!" while she wept silently, the tears trickling between closed lids and her head thrust back so that he must rise to bring it close to him. They were that way for a while, smothered in tweed and vest buttons. Then, piteously, she regarded him.

"Tony, Tony, I have hurt you so!"

He gulped, "Don't!"—and recaptured her. After that, words came, jerkily, interrupted by kisses, and not particularly logical words. By the time Nancy said, "I'm glad I hid that gun—you big gorilla!" logic was irrelevant.

Major MacArthur, having obeyed Mammy Pickett's injunction to let not appetite wait on courtesy and being not only full of food but most agreeably drunk, tried to rise, thought better of it and beamed on his daughter instead. You are, he informed her, beautiful, as beautiful as Sally Semple in her halcyon days, and he was well along on a story that had occurred to him of Mrs.

Jones Pelham's lawn party for William Jennings Bryan, when he became conscious of the fact that his son-in-law was addressing him.

"I beg your pardon?" inquired the Major.

"I was asking you, Chief, about the real estate business. We been talkin' about it, me and Nancy, upstairs; we're thinkin' about goin' into it."

The Major goggled.

"You mean, Tony, you're quitting—this?"

His apprehensive wave included the Bourbon bottle, which, he realized with a start, was still there.

Nancy leaned over and patted his arm.

"Don't worry, my pet. We won't be bone-dry. You're pretty far gone, pop, but I can't fuss at you to-night. I'll do even better than that. ... Pass his glass, Tony. Come on, Dempsey, this one is on me!"

CHAPTER TEN

SISTER CRAYCRAFT woke in light, light near and blinding, and for an instant she thought it was morning and "that" was the sun. That dissolved into an electric bulb—the filament became gigantic red cables searing her pupils, and she knew it was still night and the sun was the lamp at the other end of the couch. She moved her head outside the bright radius, the room descended black and stuffy and soundless, and Sister tried to crawl back into her dream.

The dream was like a lovely song in which she was one of the notes, bodiless and soaring. It was about Sentinel Park when she was a child. They went through meadows where daisies swung and butterflies darted above the cat-tails along green banks, and when they had trundled across the little bridge, she in the baby-buggy and Cindy pushing tranquilly behind, they came to a log hut. Cindy said the Exposition had left it there. Treasures were in the hut, rusty iron in the shape of long sticks, short sticks, big balls and little balls like heavy marbles. There was a black hat with a silver cord and on one wall a flag. She knew it was a flag, ragged though it was, for it was red and blue with stars, only it was not like the flag at home. Cindy said the iron was gunbarr'ls. Guns and bay'nets and bullets. Some of the balls were cannonballs and some Minnie balls. They were in the War, said Cindy. The War was a long time ago, but the Exposition you could almost remember. The Exposition had left the treasures, too, but the Exposition might come back for them so you had better not take them away. But you played with them there. It was better than playing with dolls. You played soldier. You picked Yankee bullets from Confederate bullets by the nicks on the ends. You raised the gun and said "Boom!" You felt the bay'nets, which were sharp once, and told Cindy the rust was blood. "Law, chile, how you talk, you oughta been a boy!" said Cindy. "Boom!" you said, and Cindy fell over dead, and you clapped your hands. Then you made Cindy do "boom" at you or stab you with a bay'net, and you were dead, and you both went over Jordan in the baby-buggy. That was down the hill, across the stream and beyond the meadows to the far side of the park. Here the sunlight fell gently among the long, white rows. Cindy wasn't scared of cemeteries like other niggers. She said this was the land of Canaan, it was Beulahland, it was the New Jerusalem, and a lot of other places you couldn't remember. The white rows were soldiers' graves, Cindy said, and when they rose they would rise in their golden uniforms on their stomping horses and the trumpets would blow. Cindy said she wanted to be there when it happened, and you did, too, and you hoped, sitting in Cindy's lap, that it would happen any minute. But it never did. You slid down in Cindy's lap and she sang. She sang "The sun shines bright" because you liked that, but mostly she sang "On the other side of Jordan 'mid the green fields of Eden" and you liked that, too, and went to sleep with the singing close yet far away, "there is rest for the weary, rest for me. . . . " It was like that when Sister was a child, and in Sister's dream it was even lovelier.

She could not crawl back into the dream. It went away so swiftly that in a minute she could remember only the vague, happy feeling of it, and in another minute that, too, went away, and the room pressed into her, the glare of the single light, the glass and the tray of cigarette butts, the stale smoky smell and the sense of being fully awake and alone. Past the dining-room, light also shone through a chink in the kitchen door, but the windows of the apartment were pitch dark so it could not be near morning.

She wondered how long she had slept. She had no headache, her head seemed quite clear and her body relaxed, lazy. Only when she stirred, warm pulses throbbed as if the blood in her veins were doubled, and she assumed that perhaps she was still drunk, for she knew she must have gone to sleep drunk. She remembered almost everything, the party, Eppy's leaving, the boys coming in, herself being very gay and not wanting any one to go. She remembered they did go, Nancy and Bo and Sally, and that she then made more drinks, for Howard and Eloise, who were dancing, and for herself. Somebody had telephoned. They were going out and meet somebody, but they all said they would have another drink first. She couldn't remember after that. She must have passed out.

Lying where the light did not bother, she decided she did not mind having passed out. They might have moved her a little—Howard and Eloise—or turned off the light or taken off her shoes. But maybe they were drunk, too. They hadn't meant to be mean—when people passed out, the rest of the party usually went right on to where it was going. She didn't mind being left alone, she was glad of it.

Motionless, she thought of her aloneness, savoring it as something cool in her parched mouth. Often she was alone, days and nights, but then she met aloneness braced against it, fighting or fleeing it as a dread guest. She would say, habitually, that she hated being alone. But she was too tired to care now—now in the thick, hushed night aloneness walked in to her like a friend, some one free of all trouble and all inquisitiveness whose calm presence obliterated the active world. Her toes found the heels of her slippers, pushed them off, and she lay with eyes closed.

A clock began striking somewhere. She thought of it as somewhere, for the chimes seemed distant and she did not identify them as the iron clock's on the mantel until they had sounded three times. She wondered if she had gone to sleep again, perhaps it was very late, and she kept count of the strokes—eight—nine—ten—eleven—why, it was only eleven o'clock! she had been asleep but a couple of hours.

Suddenly Sister decided to get up. She sat erect, swung her legs from the couch and stood in her stockinged feet. The room rotated, then steadied. She walked toward the kitchen.

The bedroom in the Craycraft apartment did not open directly into the other rooms. Where the arched entrance to the dining-room spread, a short, narrow corridor abutted to the left, and as she reached this point, Sister automatically glanced to the left to see whether the bedroom lights were on. She saw no lights because the door at the end of the corridor was closed.

She stopped. The fact of the closed door was not remarkable, nor her realization that no light showed beneath it, as would have been the case had lights been left burning. She stopped subconsciously, and she turned into the corridor in mere reaction to a suggestion that she might not be alone, after all. Every one might have gone home. Howard might have passed out, too. He might be in the bedroom.

Her hand was on the knob when she heard the voice. In that split-second between the touch of the cool metal and the moment she would have twisted it, the voice paralyzed her with the force of an explosion. Yet the voice was not loud that spoke Howard's name, it was scarcely a murmur.

The time she stood there with her hand on the knob was a little time, not more than a hundred heart-beats, yet in each beat her mind outsped her muscles as electricity outspeeds the insulation that encloses it. When she took her hand away, she had a picture of the bedroom—her bedroom—bitten on her mind to the last jot.

Yet still she stood there. Through the door she saw them, through the dark she saw them, and whatever else went on in her head of anger and grief and disgust was a storm outside a fortress, a tumult clashing on the edges of the flaming clear picture of those two, Howard and Eloise. She could not move while the picture burned.

Then, beyond the panel, something other than articulate speech flowed out to her horribly, and Sister fled.

In the living-room she hunted for a cigarette. She struck a match and lit it, her fingers shaking. The flame singed her hair, but her only response was consciousness that her hair was rough about her face. She walked to a wall-mirror and thrust back the wisps of hair, smoothing the top of her head and the back. The woman looking at her was not a woman, but a dummy which must be tidied. Its eyes were dead spots. She looked at the dummy, and the dummy looked at her, and all either saw were pictures of horrible sounds. From the couch she took her slippers, hesitated, and tucked them under one arm. She thought, "I must go to the bathroom." With that, a shudder twitched her, she turned and ran to the foyer of the apartment, where she snatched the coat lying on the small table—a man's raincoat—and stooped to put on her slippers before she opened the outer door and closed it carefully behind her.

Her impulse was to meet no one. But to walk down four flights of stairs was "silly." The elevator boy, who would be in the lobby, would be so surprised.

She pushed the button, arranging the coat around her shoulders while she listened for the elevator's hum, and when the car arrived she nodded and smiled at the boy as she entered it.

"Nice evenin', Miz Craycraft'."

"Yes, it is a fine evening, John."

The words marched back and forth in her brain like soldiers. Yes, it is a fine evening ... wheel! Yes, it is a fine evening ... wheel! It is a fine evening, John ... wheel!—left oblique! John, it is a fine evening. ... And upstairs in my room ... in my room ... in my room. ...

She walked across the lobby as unswervingly as though her purpose was not a mere hurtling toward anywhere save back yonder.

Fred Prentiss had been calling for nearly a block before she heard him. He was panting as he came up.

"Boy, did I yell at you! Where's the fire, Sister? What happened to all of you? Thought you were going to meet me at Brundage's!"

She regarded him abstractedly as though they had not just met but had been talking for some time.

"Were we? I'd forgotten."

"Well, I knew you all were drunk but I didn't think you were that drunk. I waited over an hour and then a fellow came by in a car and said he'd drop me and the nigger said you'd just left and then I saw you. But I had to holler my head off—where's the rest of the bunch?"

"They've gone," said Sister. "I don't know where they went."

Fred Prentiss was looking at her uncertainly. He took off his hat, dabbed his forehead with a handkerchief and put on his hat. He said, "Well"—and stopped.

"I'm thirsty," said Sister.

"I'm cold, too," she said.

She appeared not to be addressing a person but an echo.

"Well," repeated Fred awkwardly, "let's go get a drink. Let's"—he hesitated—"go to my place."

"All right," said Sister. She looked around. "Have you got a car?"

"But, my goodness, it's just a block!" he expostulated. "Goodnight, Sister! Don't you know where you are? I believe you are drunk."

She shook her head, and as he took her arm and they moved off through the frosty moonlight, the trembling of her arm startled him. Startled and frightened, yet pierced him with sudden, dry breathlessness.

2

Fred Prentiss turned his key in the latch, held the door open and clicked on a light as he followed Sister into his flat. He went to his bedroom and clicked on a light there and fumbled in a bureau drawer before he came out and ushered her past him. He was glad he had gotten the powder and rouge that day. The little comb, too.

When she returned to the front room, he had fetched a pitcher of icewater and placed a bowl of ice cubes, bottles and a siphon on the end-table of the couch. They gleamed dully, and he had a pleasant sense of their fitness in a bachelor's rooms.

"Shall we have a fire?" asked Fred.

"It would be nice," said Sister.

That pleased him, too. The little fire-place was no sham, it had been the irresistible attraction when first he saw the flat, and though occasions for fires were exceptional in Fred's life and only once or twice did he in solitary extravagance burn altars to the Hebes of his fancy, he kept a small store of logs against the chance of the golden reality.

"Drink?" said Fred. "Gin or Scotch? Or would you like a cocktail?"

"Scotch, please," said Sister, and Fred was glad again for Tony's advice and Tony's prompt delivery at six o'clock and his own canniness.

He had suggested this piquant tryst on the spur of the encounter and almost without belief that Sister would accept, and now that she was here, actually with him in his rooms and seated fatefully in the deep chair near the window, he still hugged his luck with a dash of incredulity and in the possibilities he formed in slow, lascivious coils, ranked this adventure as but a prelude to his party Sunday, which in turn would be preliminary to the stroke his imagination as yet could scarcely fix.

He pulled down all the shades so that he could pull down the shade behind Sister's chair, he lit the lamp beside it and snapped off the toplight. He had not quite the courage to put them in fire-light alone.

He asked her if she were comfortable.

Sister said, after a disconcerting silence: "Did you say something?"

He repeated his question, vexed that she had not even looked up but sat holding her drink and staring at the fire with her head dropped.

"I'm quite comfortable," said Sister.

On the couch, he sipped his own drink with a nonchalance assumed. There was something queer about all this, Sister hurrying along the street with no hat and an old raincoat, the disappearance of the others, her readiness to come up here and her listless manner, as if she didn't care where she went or where she was. He couldn't figure it out. She'd been drinking, of course, but she didn't seem drunk, she wasn't like Sister drunk, she seemed doped, and that was absurd. He couldn't come right out and ask her what was the matter—the ineradicable flunkey in him balked at that—yet they couldn't just sit there and say nothing.

"You don't know where Howard is?" he asked.

To his amazement, she shivered. She shivered violently, dismaying him with the fear that she was about to be sick, but immediately she lifted her highball and drank it off.

"No," she said, "I told you I didn't know. ... I think I'd like another drink, Fred."

He got it for her, more nonplused than ever. Sister usually bubbled over on a party; she was the last person in the world to give a curt answer and then huddle back pulling silently at the jug. Well, what the hell? here she was, and here he was, and the night was young. He watched her drink, her hair a nimbus against the lamp-glow, her skirt rumpled above the knee where she had flung one leg beneath the other, and the thin trickle of excitement that had begun to tap in Fred's pulses tapped faster, thickened and raced, until the quick beats in his chest were like tiny, hurting blows.

Suddenly Sister began to talk. She began with her customary drawl, the slipshod scraps of speech where laughter completes meaning, but Fred had not responded before she was pitching her sentences at him like rockets, waiting for none to explode to launch another.

"It's a crazy world, isn't it, Fred? Just like it was all jumbled together and everything in it was pulling every which way. You and me and everybody else, we're all kind of crazy, and what's the good of trying to think and decide things, what's best for you and what's best for somebody else? because what's fine for you may be just rotten for somebody else, and the other way 'round. Don't you think that's so, Fred? I know it's so—you certainly can't get anywhere thinking, you've got to do something! But suppose you don't know what to do? Suppose you're in a mess where anything you do'll look wrong—wrong for you, that is—it's bound to make you unhappy—and the other person, well, you can't possibly know what'll make them happy and what won't, only you know the way things are you're both unhappy and it's all wrong—well, what do you do, Fred?"

She went on without waiting for an answer.

"I'm pretty silly, I guess. I reckon I ought not to think at all, I ought not to do anything at all. About things. Let 'em rip—that's the idea, isn't it? Just let 'em rip. ... You mustn't think 'm talking about anything in particular, either. I'm not. Just things in general, you know, the way things are and the way people are, some happy and some not happy, but most of them unhappy. They are unhappy, don't you think—almost everybody?"

And when Fred only gaped at her—"They used to say 'be good and you'll be happy,' but I don't believe that, I never did believe it. Besides, what's good and what isn't? Maybe the bad people aren't bad, maybe they just want things like the good people do and they go and do something about it. The good people don't. They're afraid to do anything, that's all. And being afraid isn't being good, is it? Maybe that's the answer. Maybe if you do what you want, you're just as good as anybody else and better off, too. But if what you want to do isn't what somebody else wants to do, and your being happy depends on their wanting the same thing you do, well, you're licked. You're just licked, aren't you, Fred?"

He shook his head helplessly, and Sister repeated, not looking at him but staring into the bottom of her glass, "I'm pretty silly."

"Do you want another drink?" Fred said.

She nodded and he got it for her.

"Look," said Sister. She leaned forward, smiling. "Look—I'm just being silly. I'm talking crazy—not about anything in particular—you know that, don't you, Fred?"

"Sure," said Fred, "sure," and because she was at once so distressed and so provocative, he said, swallowing. "It's all right—everything's going to be all right."

Sister laughed.

"Everything's going to be all right," she repeated, and suddenly she froze again, crouched back into the chair with her head drooped and the firelight licking over it and up and down the slacked lines of her leg and thigh. And though he stammered into a feeble disquisition on morals, declaring that he agreed with her, intelligent people didn't bother about morals any more, the only morals were expediency, you were a fool if you didn't take your fun where you found it—and all this with a vague notion that he was weakening her defenses and slipping past her guard—he could get no reply from her, not so much as a nod, and in the middle of a word he stopped talking, letting the word die in his throat as one might indifferently let a gnat die, and sat drawn together on the couch with his eyes fastened, pale and gluttonous, on her sloped figure.

He was painfully excited. He did not understand his luck at all, what she was driving at or what was the matter behind this business, and he gave it up, he let all that fade away from him, but the room and the fire and the enticement of the figure in the deep chair, he let those caress him in a warm wave of physical delight. Where her stocking ended above the knee, he could see the white flesh, a mere feather in the shadow, but he was acutely aware of it and the sight thrust his own flesh sharp and formidable into his consciousness so that he was sensible of the prickle of sweat above his lips and of each hair on the back of his hands. He touched one hand with the other, and the stroke of his own fingers was exquisite to him.

Somewhere in a book he had read of just such a scene as this, and he thought back carefully, recalling exactly what the man had done. He had sat down on the floor beside the girl, stroking the girl's hand slowly, her hand first and then her bare arm, until between them ran a magnetic, sensuous current. After a while he had begun to kiss her hand and arm, slowly, insinuatingly, drugging her with kisses. It had been precisely like this in the book, a room and firelight and a man and a girl, only it had been raining, too, the steady drone of rain on St. Valentine's Eve. . . .

Fred got up and walked to the end-table. He fiddled with the ice-cubes, left them and went to his victrola. At the first cry of the violins, Sister stirred.

"Don't, please," she said, "I couldn't bear it if they played that!"

She couldn't have known what the record was—he wondered what she thought it was—but he stopped the machine and stood looking at her, a tingling in his fingers and his chest hurting.

"The lamp," said Sister. "Hurts my eyes."

She herself reached up and flicked the cord. Darkness and firelight ran together, each blacker and brighter than before, and Fred lowered himself to the rug beside the chair. Her hand was there. He took it, lightly, and lightly brushed his fingers along the palm, along the wrist and up the inner curve of the limp arm. Then he began to kiss the hand and arm. The hurting and the tingling increased in him as he pressed closer to the chair, as his body touched and pressed her body, and now was no distinction in his mind—no fire or room or hand, no Sister even, or any image of woman out of past fantasies—only a great flame of lust that was all self, that was all "I."

Sister moved her head. Her lips dug into the chair's velvet as though their preservation somehow was important. But nothing was important any more...nothing. It was horrible to be huddled here like this, and then to be stumbling along into the bedroom with some one holding your hand—Cindy used to hold your hand when you went to bed—but it wasn't important, it didn't matter...nothing mattered any more....

CHAPTER ELEVEN

THERE ARE pennants and cheering in the streets, and in the windows yellow, white and bronze chrysanthemums, big as moons. Hawkers pace the congested sidewalks, waving sheaves of pennants, thrusting up boards on which the ribbons flutter bravely under pigmy footballs. The purple of the University. The white and scarlet of Tech. Cars whoop by with the pennants streaming, the ribbons glow with the 'mums on the breasts of pretty girls, and over the crowds, the colors, the Saturday noon, the sun shines bright.

Howard Craycraft walked gloomily toward the hotel where the University team was staying. About the entrance and in the lobby men swarmed, coagulating suddenly into clumps, melting, swirling together again, but never halting long in that nervous, questing impatience of all football crowds. Where the groups were quietest there was betting, but mostly the swarm was noisy, young men jostling arrogantly, older men slapping backs and retreating to corners where flasks clinked; a band played thunderously on the mezzanine, and occasionally a Tech student overfiery or already made a conqueror by com gloated into jubilee with a long "Ye-e-e-up! Oh—

> "Palms of victory!
> Palms of glo-o-ry!
> Palms of victoree
> We—shall—wave!"

Howard saw men he knew. He paused to hail forgotten chaps he'd been in school with, fraternity brothers charged him and introduced him to undergraduates—"Brother Craycraft, Brother Miles," and the quick lunge above the grip—he laid twenty dollars with Greek Sam on the University by two touchdowns and had a drink of something Runt Hughes called "gobbler." "One shot of this, boy, and you talk turkey!" Gradually his morose depression lifted; he was with the boys, jaunty with the jaunty.

Here, where the sanguine male dominated, he could persuade himself that his anxiety was nonsense. He had been a fool to lie awake last night, fighting it, and to go to the office this morning with the specter grisly at his side. She didn't know a thing—probably she didn't have the slightest suspicion.

After all, he told himself, why should she suspect? Just because, when they came out of the room, she was gone, didn't spell a thing. On the contrary, her absence meant everything was all right. Undoubtedly, this was what happened: she woke up, she was still pickled or just sober enough to decide nobody was home, she figured they'd gone to Sally's, or somewhere, and so she hustled out after them. Probably she thought to catch them downstairs, or something.

That was it. If she'd messed around, pickled and all, he would have heard her. Wasn't he listening? Sure he was, he was listening all the time; he had been careful as hell. And if she'd come as far as the bedroom door, what of it? She wouldn't have heard anything then—they were both careful as hell, they'd been mighty quiet about it—and the door was locked. She'd have figured, even if she heard something, that he was in there, that he was alone and locking her out as he had before. Shucks, he'd been silly to get scared!

And he wouldn't have, either, if Eloise hadn't got funny when they came out and found her gone, if Eloise hadn't gotten scared herself and insisted on lighting out then and there. Well, that was all right by him, too. Love 'em and leave 'em. Watch out, dear, you'll break your god damn neck. ... Usually you had to go through a lot of mush, afterwards. It was all right by him to dump Eloise at the Chapmans' front door.

Of course, he didn't know for sure that Sister went to Chapmans'—that she spent the night there. But undoubtedly that was what she did—she might have passed out, and they put her to bed, and it was too late to telephone him. Or maybe they tried to telephone while he was on his way with Eloise and they couldn't get him. When Eloise walked in—well, Eloise would be smart enough to dope up some good lie.

She must have gone to Chapmans', he repeated. Where else would she go? Once, when she walked out on him, she went home to mother. And once, after her mother was dead, she had spent the night at a hotel. They had quarreled those times about nothing—about nothing, he insisted. And this time there wasn't that much, not even a quarrel. Shucks, she couldn't have known anything; she beat it, she went to Chapmans', she passed out, and Sally put her to bed. That was all there was to it.

"Brother Craycraft—Brother Zarner—"

"I said a drink, not a bath, pal, old pal, old pal—"

"—wanted ten dollars for all night and I said sure in a pig's—"

"—victoree! We—shall—wave!"

Of course, he might have called up the Chapmans this morning. But suppose she hadn't been there—suppose she'd gone to some other girl's house—she might have—that would look fine, wouldn't it? calling up to ask if anybody, had seen his wife! She would have liked that—his calling up the Chapmans when she wasn't there—paging her all over town—she'd have been sore as hell if he'd done that. ... "I can look out for myself!" Sure you can. I wasn't going to humiliate you by chasing you all over town. ...

Funny she hadn't called him this morning. But that didn't spell a thing, either. If she was drunk, she must have slept late. Besides, he'd been out of the office a lot this morning. Maybe she had called and they just forgot to tell him. Maybe she was calling him right now. All right, let her ring. Why should he hang around a telephone? waiting her pleasure . . . when she hadn't thought to call him last night . . . or early this morning . . . when he didn't know where she was . . . worrying about her. . . . Shucks, let her ring!

"Brother Craycraft—Brother Scott—Brother Scott's on the team—"

Over the clumps of heads he saw Bo's tall shoulders, he yelled "Bo!" and Bo turned, and smiled. The crowd swirled, coagulated, shutting and opening. They met under the stairs, the band thunderous above.

"Let's get out of here."

"Can't, Howard. Gotta see a man about a dog first."

"All right. I'll wait."

"No, don't. We gotta get started. We gotta get the girls started."

"Well, we've already got the tickets—"

"What? I can't hear anything you say! You go ahead and get Sister started and come by for us."

Howard hesitated.

"Well, if you make it snappy—my car's outside—"

"What?" shouted Bo again. "I've got my car. We'll go in mine. You go ahead and get 'em started."

He waved himself on, the crowd sifted between them, and Howard, after an irresolute moment, pushed toward the entrance.

But his depression stalked him. Funny Bo hadn't said anything about last night. Funny he hadn't mentioned Sister's being there. Still, that didn't spell a thing. You couldn't talk with that band going. You couldn't hear yourself think. Sister must be home by now. He'd do what Bo said. He'd go ahead and get her started. . . .

2

Sister looked up from a chair by the window where she was drying her hair in the sunshine and manicuring her fingernails.

"Hello," said Howard.

"Hello," she said.

She went on filing her nails.

He had taken off his hat but not his overcoat, dropping his hat on the hall-table and walking in briskly, his hands in his coat-pockets, his air that of a man in a hurry but unperturbed. The sight of her brought him sharp relief, yet he was at once made uncomfortable by her mere presence. Without a glance or a word exchanged, she roused in him his guilt and the necessity for exercising it.

"Gee," he said, "not dressed yet? You better get a hustle on!"

He had not looked at her directly, nor approached her, covering his uneasiness with a quick stride around the room, dropping into a chair because striding about might appear nervous, drumming with his fingers and then ceasing to drum.

He said, "Where's Lavinia?"

"I let her go," said Sister.

She was in the light robe she usually wore mornings, but she looked fresh and very dainty as though she had recently stepped from the tub and been diligent before her mirror, and Howard knew from experience that the business of slipping on clothes can be comparatively brief once a woman has completed the preliminaries.

"You better get dressed, hadn't you?" he urged.

Sister laid aside her file and picked up the buffer. She had not looked up again, and she did not look up now, and Howard's front of bland innocence began to sour.

"Look here, Sister, we haven't got—"

"I'm not going to the game," she said quietly.

He forced himself to stare at her, as if by sheer optical energy he could lift her out of her seat, into garments and onto a stadium.

"Not going to the game? Don't be silly. I've had these tickets for weeks. We're all going together, Bo and Sally and—the rest. They're waiting for us to come by for them."

The buffer halted.

"I'm not going," she said. "I don't feel very well. Please, Howard"—she was speaking slowly, like an actress rehearsing lines, yet with an evident effort to conciliate him—"I don't want to seem—peculiar, but—I really can't go."

He continued to stare at her, and now he felt an overwhelming desire for her to look at him. He had not cared to see her eyes before, but now he must see her eyes, he must see what was in them, she must not hide her eyes and what they held.

"Well—see here—I think it's mighty funny. You were so keen to go. You were keen last night. We were all talking about it, and you were the one who was crazy to go. I think it's mighty funny you're backing out now."

"I know," said Sister. "I'm sorry."

"Well, why don't you go? Come on—dash into your clothes. You'll feel better after you get out in the air."

"No," said Sister. "No ... I couldn't, anyway, now, with my hair all wet."

"Well, it's a helluva time to wash your hair!"

She shrank against the chair, and suddenly Howard saw her eyes, unlashed and naked.

"You go on, Howard. You go on and have a good time."

It was like looking into the core of all the trouble he had ever known. It was as though he had never looked into eyes before. He saw their sockets, the blue tinge of the skin beneath them, the lines sketched lightly from the corners of the lids, the whites veined a little with red, these items summing up to the realization that she did not look well for a fact, and he saw past the outer structure, the iris, the cornea, the retina, into a structure without bottom. On this he closed his own eyes, quickly, turning his head before he opened them again, and the trouble that lay in that bottomless chasm he put from him.

Howard got up.

"Well, if you're going to be hard-headed—I'll have the devil of a time explaining to Bo and Sally. It's damned embarrassing, you know, when a party's all set and somebody stands up the rest at the last minute. Still, if you're really sick, I suppose there's nothing to be done about it."

"I'm sorry," said Sister again. "Tell them I have a bad headache. Tell them I have a hangover. That won't sound funny, will it?"

Howard studied her furtively, looking as if he wanted to say something. But whatever it was, he could not get it out. He laughed instead.

"I'll say it won't!" he sneered.

He strolled across the room, pulling gloves out of his pocket and striking them with one hand against the other. But at the door he turned.

"Look, Sister—you don't want me to stay here with you, do you?"

She remembered that for some time after he had gone. She would lose it, temporarily, in the gray floods rolling over her, but it would come back, bobbing up like a chip refusing to sweep out with the tide—he had offered to give up the game and stay with her—and she would seize it, cherishing it, making the most of it, trying to pretend that he would have liked to stay if she had nodded and not answered, "No, indeed, I'll be all right." And this would comfort her a little; it was still something after the gray floods redoubled, after she gave up the pretense and admitted the futility of his staying if he had stayed ... for what? To sit and stare at her? To crush her with his glum silence or stab her with hard evasions? To face his questions? Why, he had not cared enough to ask them! To confess, then, and receive his confession ... and bring down on them such shattering as never, she knew, could be cleared away. No, in books and plays and even in real life, somewhere, they might forgive and start again, these wise people who can manipulate love as if love were a Ford automobile to be steered or stopped or kept in the garage. But she couldn't. Love to her had been a simple thing—like a candle that stayed lighted without your bothering—and gradually it had become something else, intricate and lost in the dark. Love cried in the dark. And she cried with it, lost.

She finished her hands. Never had she been so scrupulous, searching microscopically for the most innocent speck. So had she bathed. So had she combed and brushed her hair. To be clean, scoured to her very memory—it was imperative. But at last even the mirror at the back of her neck could offer no more vents to energy; she put it down and laid her hands together in her lap. The thumb of one hand she caught in the grip of the other, an old habit that went back, perhaps, to childhood and Cindy walking with her through the green meadows.

There was no sound in the apartment, and sounds from the street, automobile horns and once singing and a cheer, penetrated faintly. The sun fed the hush, pouring into the room its impalpable floods of gold. They should have shouted. In their unchanging, mute descent, they were unreal. Sister reached up and lowered the shade. The radiance dimmed to dusty orange, and she rose, trembling.

3

Cold had come with the twilight, closing over the stands and the ranks of automobiles packed along the sidelines, over the boys shivering in the treetops and the college buildings cold against the cold sky. The stands sent out a rhythmic thump of feet, thousands of chilled feet pounding in unison the chilled stone, and a steady chant from thousands of muffled throats—"Touchdown,

Tech, touchdown, Tech"—like the exhaust of a giant locomotive laboring in the gloom. Only at one end of the field, where shadows writhed against the earth, did cold seem to hold off.

"Touchdown, Tech," mumbled Howard, crouched on the folded top of Bo's car.

"You fool—root for the University!"

A whistle blew; the shadows raced in the mist; the chant of the giant broke to a roar—the whistle blew; the shadows, writhing, were infinitesimal beside the heaving stands.

"It's over! ... Come on, let's see if we can get out of here. Kiss your money good-by, Howard, they'll never score again now."

All along the packed rows, motors began to sputter and lights to pierce the darkness. Horns and backfire competed with the cheers, the lights wove and crisscrossed in blinding patterns—the whistle blew and the crowd struck, rushing, inundating, before a dozen cars had climbed the slope and gone winking across the campus toward College Street.

"We'll never get out now ... Goddamit. ... "

"Who gives a cuss? Let's have another drink. Where's the bottle, Eloise?"

She handed him the bottle and Howard drank, worming down on his spine in his corner of the car.

Eloise moved closer under the laprobe. The cold had come into the car, possessing them, coming through the robe, coming between them where their sides pressed in unfeeling union.

"Drink, Eloise ... 's gobbler. One shot of this and you talk turkey. Hey, Bo—wanna drink?"

No answer from the front, where Bo drove tortuously and Sally drove with him, her muscles contracting, relaxing, contracting with each thrust of clutch and brake. Eloise tilted the bottle. Hellfire split her gullet, but she caught her breath and waited the slow, spreading waves of warmth. She handed the bottle silently to Howard; he drank again and they huddled, wordless, glued, insensate, while the car crawled on up the interminable slope.

In College Street, the Tech nightshirt parade already was moving, a turbulence of white and scarlet under jets of arc-light, and they moved behind it, rocked by a wake of band music and cheers. Howard shook his bottle and shouted at the Tech students.

"Who wrecked Tech? Who wrecked Tech? An' a big Uuuuuuu—wrecked Tech!"

"Ya-a-a-ah! What's the score, pal? Where you been all my life, old pal, old pal? Give 'im the score, men! One!—two!—three!—four—"

Howard stood up in the car, his lips puckered, but they drowned him out with boos and yells and whistles, and he fell back laughing, and the others laughed, and so they swung into Cherokee Avenue part of the parade and continued with it to the building where the Craycrafts lived.

The cold did not matter now. They could mock it in the first blast of steam heat, as they stood before the Craycrafts' door, waiting for Howard to find his key, they could slap their hands and playfully shove each other and call for the St. Bernards.

"Sister!" they called. "The St. Bernards!"

Sister did not answer, and Howard, who went first, turning on lights, stopped his length from the chair. Though she was curled in it not unnaturally, one foot tucked beneath her and her arm slack, there was no missing the hole in her head and the pistol—his pistol—on the floor. He would weep when he read her note—"Good-by, Howard honey, please don't be mad at me, the blues just got me"—but he would never forgive her her open eyes.

CHAPTER TWELVE

WHEN THE children departed for Sunday school and she had discussed dinner with cook, Sally Chapman at last could think about the awfulness of it. She had been too stunned and too harassed before to think, going through all those motions last night and this morning with no more cerebration than a dog employs in scratching fleas. Now she was alone, now she could summon the awfulness, stark and irrevocable. And immediately the most awful part, she discovered, was the realization that it was going to make so little difference.

Her best friend was dead, and here she was, unchanged, shepherding her family, directing her household, debating Russian dressing or mayonnaise, doing everything as she had done it yesterday and the day before and the day before that. Here she was, contemplating trees and sky as bright as ever that should be black with tears because Sister would look upon them nevermore. That is the real terror of Death, thought Sally—and she thought this as profoundly as the first philosopher to behold the terror stalking through the primal murk—you die and all other life goes on. Things go on. Her telephone would ring, and she would answer it, and save that she would think, unthinking, "That is Sister," and it would never be Sister, the world would be the same. Presently the weight on her heart would lighten, even the missing feeling would go away, and when she thought of Sister, though the thought would be sad, it would not be nearly so important as Buddy's clean handkerchief or Marcia's cough or a choice of salad dressings.

She forced herself to grieve, to pin her thoughts on Sister. Suicide!—dreadful when it is a stranger in a newspaper head- line, inconceivable for a friend. The shock to them all, rushing in gayly from the gay night. Howard's cry—poor Howard!—and his agony, almost unendurable to witness. But his agony had been more tolerable than his fury when he whirled on them, shouting at Eloise, shouting those dreadful accusations.

Sally shut her eyes. She would not think about that. She hoped she would not think about Eloise ever again. She would think about Sister.

Why should Sister kill herself? Of all the people Sally knew, Sister had seemed the happiest. Sister had laughed at her troubles and was always trying to kid other people out of theirs. "Life's too short," she used to say, "life's too short to fret." And then a girl like that, a jolly girl, a laughing girl with no cares and no respon- sibilities, with every reason to live, killed herself. Why?

"Liquor," Bo had said last night after they got home. "She never would have done it, Mama, if she hadn't been drinking so hard."

But Sally, weeping in his arms, found no understanding and no solace. We all drink, and some of us drink hard, but we do not kill ourselves, not we who drink out of sheer sociability and good fellowship. Only sodden drunkards kill themselves, not our best friends.

Sister wasn't drunk, Sister wasn't crazy, Sister was simply unhappy. "The blues just got me," she had written, and Sally shuddered, thinking that all the time Sister was laughing and being jolly, she was unhappy, that all the time she kidded, the blues were getting her.

Sister was your best friend and you didn't really know her. You saw Sister every day and you thought Sister told you every- thing. But Sister had secrets you never dreamed, Sister suffered when you were completely blind to her suffering, Sister was kill- ing herself at the moment you were laughing and singing, when maybe if you had been a better friend, if you had been a little more observing and a little more sympathetic, if you had said something, only a word or two—

Sally buried her head in her arms and bawled.

"You'll feel better for a good cry." ... Well, she did feel better. She sat up and wiped her eyes.

Of course, Howard was the reason. A man was always the cause of a woman's unhappiness. Damn them—why couldn't women get along without men? Some women did. Ernestine Hill did, though even Ernestine would rather play golf with a man than a woman. Eppy Spurlock got along without a man for thirty years, but that was because no man wanted Eppy; as soon as one did, Eppy chucked her job, her folks and everything else for the man. Well, I'm glad she landed him, thought Sally.

The bitterness was not so much in wanting a man as in losing him. You have him, you put yourself completely into him and his, you grow to depend on him and believe he depends on you, and then you lose him as Sister did. You wake up to discover you've been a fool. "No man is worth it." No? What else have you got now that you no longer have your man? ... A woman makes a great mistake to sink herself in her children, her home, her man. The children grow up and leave her, the male child because he is a male and the female child because she, too, must have her man. Some women realize that. Modern women like Mrs. Carver. They have something else, a business, a hobby, some interest besides their men. Why don't you get a hobby? Suppose Bo—died? quit?

Quailing, Sally dully thought: "I must do something ... interests ... what interests? ... that old wood-burning set. It's somewhere in the attic—'artistic' ... They all said you were artistic. ... "

They had said nothing to Eloise, afterward. They had said nothing about Eloise to each other. She and Bo, sitting inert, silent, in their bedroom.

Then Eloise had come in.

"I'm so upset. You people...darlings!...but I can't stay. I—I'm quite sick over this."

They had looked at her, voiceless.

"Bo, will you get my ticket for me?"

"Of course, Eloise."

"I don't want to be impolite, but—if there's a train tonight—or to-morrow—"

"I'll 'phone the station right away," Bo had said.

So Eloise was at the station now. Bo was putting her on the train, the train would go away, and they would never see Eloise again. Never, never, never again! She would not write to Eloise, and if Eloise wrote to her, she would tear the letter up and not even read it. She would forget Eloise, she would not even hate her any more, and what Eloise had done to Sister and to all of them would become vague after a while, would not make any difference.

Sally spread her damp handkerchief on the back of a chair. She went to the bathroom and washed her eyes with boric acid, she changed from a housedress into a frock, she hunted for a bunch of old keys and started toward the attic stairs. But, at their foot, she heard cook calling.

"Does you want onions in de salad, Miz Chapman?"

"No—yes! Wait a minute, Ada. I'm coming right down."

And life went on, in other places, for other people—where Howard Craycraft bowed to the undertaker's thumb, poised like an obsequious but proud flunky on the illuminated page of the casket catalogue; where Major Wallace MacArthur raised his voice from the Sunday paper as Nancy's spoon halted halfway between her grapefruit and her mouth; where Fred Prentiss, the paper at his feet, stared at the deep chair until vainglory drenched, suddenly, the sick fear in his throat; and where Eppy Spurlock sat alone in her Pullman section, oblivious to life pelting past.

Her feet, in their new oxfords, reposed like sedate little nesting ducks on a green footcushion (she had been embarrassed when the porter brought it, but her short legs were more comfortable thus braced), her hands clasped each other damply, her head rested firm against the white slip-cover at her back, and her gaze for an hour had not shifted from a perspective in which the only animate object was her new hat swinging from an upper hook.

She, too, might have read in the bulk of print beside her that Hoover Predicts Prosperity, Steel Hits New Low, Breadlines Grow, Holy Cross Swamps Harvard, and then on an inside page, that Mrs. Howard Craycraft, wife of the prominent young realtor, had died during the night from a heart attack, leaving a host of friends—influential friends who could suppress suicides, the account might have added—to mourn her and to sympathize with her husband, son of the late Governor Craycraft, in his great bereavement.

But Eppy, since leaving Corinth and recovering from her family's kisses, commands and warnings, their reproaches for not letting them come along, their relief that she was off their hands at last, their anxiety lest she miss the way to the altar, and their eagerness to descend on her as soon as she had trod it—Eppy Spurlock, fiancée of Jocelyn Randolph, had no eyes for world cataclysms or private griefs. Hers was an inward vision, and whatever she saw there, of gems and garlands or darker mysteries, they completely absorbed her.

"First call to lunch—diner up ahead," a voice had droned some time before.

She had not moved.

Figures passing, lurching, bumping, murmured, "Pardon me."

She did not notice them.

"Eppy Spurlock!"

She gave a little jump, the spectacles coruscated.

"Eloise King!"

Each bewilderedly surveyed the other.

"Well, I declare, Eloise! Whatever are *you* doing here?"

"Going to New York. But I didn't know *you* were on this train!"

A mutual note of pained surprise. In the faces of both something like dismay, Eppy's the frank regret of a child shaken to duty from a dream of taffy trees, Eloise's a wariness and a glint under her buttery smile. Yet, to the other passengers, merely two friends well met.

"Well, I declare!" repeated Eppy. "Sit down, Eloise."

Eloise sat down. She had to, unless she wanted to block the aisle or rudely march on. Eppy furtively kicked the footcushion out of sight, and both beamed with that air of pleased assurance two women always display when they don't know what to say next.

Eloise said she supposed Eppy was on her way to meet the bridegroom and Eppy said yes, she was.

Eppy said she had no idea Eloise was returning to New York so soon, and Eloise said she hadn't either until they telegraphed her last night that rehearsals must start immediately. My new play, you know.

She watched Eppy.

Eppy said how nice, you didn't tell me at Sister's party you wrote plays.

"I don't. I act in them," said Eloise.

"Oh," said Eppy. "It was a cute party, wasn't it? I think Sister's too sweet for anything."

Eloise, watching, seemed to let her breath go.

"Yes, she is," said Eloise.

Suddenly she was glad of Eppy, glad of somebody to talk to and to talk to her. Anybody. Eppy Spurlock was a gabby fool. Thank God for gabby fools!

Deliberately, she said: "Is what's-his-name, Mr. Randolph, meeting you at the train?"

Now, while Eppy gushed, she could relax, now she could lean back without listening and challenge her own thoughts. With Sally and Bo she had been afraid, and by herself she had been afraid, but with Eppy, who knew nothing and would gabble about nothing, she was secure. Come out, Shame, and face me! You cannot live in the same body with my vanity. While a fool gabbles, we will settle this once and for all. ... Well, what is at the bottom of it? Merely this: you discovered what they always told you, that New York is the beginning and end of civilization and a New Yorker venturing among the interior tribes gets scalped.

It was as simple as that to Eloise—she felt scalped. She could take every incident of her stay in Corinth, from a child's aloofness to drunken kisses, and rationalize them into futile attempts on her part to be a good Indian. She could take each person she had met, the women she had patronized and the men she had chased, and judge them barbarians, including the moron who killed herself and then tried to put the blame on her, embarrassing her and spoiling her trip. She could tell herself, finally, that though the breadlines shiver before St. Vincent's and the radiators clank coldly in a thousand Village walkups, the brightest sun still shines over Broadway and one New York cocktail is worth all the ripe corntops in Dixie.

She could and she did. No shame was in her now. She was going back, thank God! to God's own godless city, and she would forget Corinth save for that rankling sense of the unpaid grudge.

"What?" she snapped to Corinth's surviving reminder.

Eppy had come to a pause and she was looking at Eloise expectantly, her gaze bright out of misty pinkness.

"I said—would you like to see Jocelyn's picture?"

Eloise threw back her head, laughing her tinny laugh.

"Good Lord! do we have to look at it now? I'm starving!— let's go in and eat."

She rose briskly, and Eppy obediently followed.

Eppy's round face was crestfallen. She would have enjoyed opening her new bag with its fittings and its breath of expensive perfume and the photograph carefully tucked among silky folds. Eloise was such an abrupt person. She was afraid of Eloise, yet afraid, too, that Eloise would abruptly leave her. Then she would have no one to talk to. So she hurried along, too concerned over keeping up with Eloise to mind the bored passengers who smiled at her agitated, crumpled rear.

In the diner were only a few people, a couple lingering over coffee, a solitary old gentleman, and, at the far end, two men together.

Eppy, though her back was to the two men, wished Eloise hadn't picked the next table. She could feel their stares, and she was embarrassed for Eloise, who must face them.

But Eloise didn't seem to mind. Eloise went right on smiling and talking and giving orders to the waiter, with now and then a flick of eyelids towards the two men, and Eppy soon forgot them in the rush of autumn hills through the broad windows and the exciting sense, keener here than in the other cars, of rushing somewhere herself.

"I love traveling, don't you, Eloise? Oh, I'm going to adore it, going to Europe!"

The men behind her were getting up, and she waited, watching Eloise's eyes, until she was sure they were out of the diner.

"What?" said Eloise.

"I said I hate men like that, the way they look at you."

"How do they look at you? I thought they were rather nice, especially the one in gray."

Eloise was smiling.

"Oh, you know—sort of bold and—possessive."

"Well, how does your wonderful Jocelyn look at you?"

"That's different."

Eppy was misty pink again, and Eloise threw back her head.

"Lord, Eppy, you're a scream!" Smiling her buttery smile, she fixed malicious eyes on the other's, which were blinking rapidly, a shy, frightened blink. "Go on, Eppy," she said, "tell me about Sonny Boy."

At five o'clock, in Compartment A, the man in gray said: "I hope you don't mind my not asking your friend? She didn't look exactly clubby."

"Good, Lord, no! I'm only too glad to be rid of her. She's been talking my bead off for hours."

Eloise watched him remove the wrappings of the bottle and expertly insert a cork-screw. Johnny Walker. And that bag didn't come from west of Fifth Avenue, either.

"She certainly is a scream, though," said Eloise. "Imagine— she's told everybody in Corinth she's going to New York to be married, and I'm convinced she invented the whole story, bridegroom and all. Why, she showed me his picture and if he isn't some radio crooner she never saw in her life, then I'm crazy!"

"Rudy Vallee?" said the man in gray.

"No, but it's somebody like that. I remember seeing that face somewhere and it was something about radio."

The man in gray set out glasses and White Rock.

"Aren't her friends on?"

"You should see her friends!" said Eloise. She added, "No, they're not—yet."

"You from Corinth?" asked the man in gray.

"Good Lord, no! When!"—said Eloise.

CHAPTER THIRTEEN

MEADOWS CRUSTED with sooty ice flashed tirelessly under harsh billboards and the wet sky, until it seemed the train must race forever through monotony. Then stone jaws closed on the tracks, wiping out the day, and the sudden roar of the tunnel flattened into a steadily, deep snarl. Eppy put her fingers to her ears, waiting for the drums to burst; but they didn't, the pressure lightened and she took her fingers away as other passengers moved into the aisle. A few moments later, while she was still tugging at her gloves, they were in the Pennsylvania Station.

In the bustle she missed Eloise. She looked around, but a redcap had caught up her bags, the crowd thrust at her, she nodded to the negro to go ahead and they went with the crowd, enveloped and carried along by it. The passengers shuffled on the stairs in a final congealment of fraternity, popping at the top into rivulets that streamed this way and that toward their separate ruts that would never join again.

Eppy stood for a second, peering at the vaulted roof, catching her breath. "Taxi," she said to the redcap, and they went, a rivulet of two. In the cab she sat bolt upright as it boomed with other taxis up the incline. She was still breathless, still in the sweep of the crowd, more than ever where the traffic leaped at them flash-bang and they leaped with it into the pellmell of Seventh Avenue on a drizzly morning. She had given the driver the name of the hotel where she had stayed briefly last Summer before she found a boarding-house near Columbia University, but the tremendous city confused her and, when the cab careened to a final stop, she must lean forward, inquiring "Are you sure?" before she saw the insignia on the doorman, waiting with his majestic umbrella.

Crossing the lobby, she felt again the surge of excitement from the palms and marble and strangers around her, and her breathlessness continued through the transaction with the clerk, whom she remembered and archly smiled at, and through the ascension to her room and the business of watching the bellboy desposit her bags and fiddle with lights and windows until she had tipped him and he had closed the door and she was alone in the profound isolation of a comfort that lacked nothing and offered nothing, left like the last soul on earth above a universe touching her only with remotest echoes.

It was a nice room. It had a bureau, a desk, a bed with a dark silk coverlet, a bedstand with a lamp on it, and another lamp beside an easy chair. The bellboy had lit this lamp because the day was dark. It shed a soft light on the room, on the cream walls, the soft hangings at the window and the dark rug on which her feet made no sound.

She opened her bags, went to the bathroom and washed, examining with interest the fixtures, the small oblongs of soap, the slit over the washbowl marked "razor blades" and the cork-screw and bottle opener clamped to the walk On the bathroom door was a sign, "Rules for Guests," and she read them all, through the one requesting guests not to bring intoxicating liquors into the hotel.

While she read, ghosts of gone, roistering males leered from the tiles, and she returned quickly to the other room and took out her things. She hung some in the closet and laid others daintily in drawers. She wished her trunk would come so she could empty it, too.

The empty bags she carried to the closet. On top the bureau she arranged her toilet articles and placed the photograph in its silver frame cater-cornered toward the back, exactly as she had kept it on her dressing-table at home. She stood off, impersonally examining it, approached and changed its position slightly, and looked about her for something else to straighten. There was nothing else.

She sat for a while in the easy chair, surveying the room in the lamp-glow and smoothing a handkerchief across her damp palms. Then she went to the desk. On it were envelopes and writing paper and several picture postcards of the hotel. She adjusted a postcard in front of her, dipped the pen and, after tracing aimless stencils on the blotter, restored the pen to the inkstand and the postcard, unmarked, to the rack.

She wished her trunk would come. In the trunk were the letters. All of them save the last one. She went to the bureau and took this out, opened it and reread it. When she had finished, she read it again, replaced it slowly in the envelope and both in the bureau drawer, went back to the desk and seated herself before a blank sheet of paper. She sat there for a long time, the pen in her fingers and her eyes fixed on the paper, but she wrote nothing.

She put away the pen. She wandered about the room, from the desk to the bed to the window. She drew the window-curtains back and stared at a roof some distance below, the tall buildings opposite and the receding New York skyline. She was not sure what part of the city that was. Her room last Summer had been on a different side. She thought it must be Times Square because of the signs, but they were illegible in rain and distance. The rain fell steadily, the drops striking the pane and trickling down to vanish off the stone ledge. The ledge was dirty and smoke rose sluggishly through the rain.

She wished her trunk would come. Leaving the window, she twisted the easy chair in the direction of the door and sat down again. But after a moment she jumped up and returned to the window. This time she stared longest at the buildings opposite as though she expected some signal, some wave of a hand. The buildings were too far away, too veiled by rain. Opaque lights shone indifferently in their indifferent sides.

Wheeling, Eppy moved with decision. The telephone was on the stand by the bed, and beneath it the thick directory. She spread the directory on the bed, standing over it and slowly turning the pages ... M ... P ... R. ... She stooped closer, turning more slowly ... Randolph. Half a column of Randolphs. ... Her forefinger crept down the page, stopped, wavered on, came back. There was a James Randolph. There was a John Randolph. There was no name between those names.

Eppy straightened, her head jerked on her spine. Well, my goodness, what did you expect? She laughed hysterically.

In the hall outside, something moved and the knock came clarion in the small, hushed room.

"Yes!" cried Eppy. "Yes!—yes!"

Her hand was at her throat.

"Come in!" she called, and the porter entered with her trunk.

"Put it there," said Eppy.

She dropped her hand.

2

After the man had left, after she had unpacked the trunk and put away the last knickknack, Eppy decided to go out. Her watch said half-past twelve. She had eaten nothing since early breakfast on the train. She must have lunch. She always had lunch.

Changing her dress and putting on the new hat, she locked the door and walked briskly to the elevator. She had stuck the key in her handbag and did not stop at the desk downstairs but proceeded directly to the hotel's dining-room. Here she ordered and ate—studying each item on the menu and chewing slowly every mouthful—canapé of caviar, consommé, chicken à la king and a chocolate éclair. She had a demi-tasse, sipping it from the spoon. She poured a second cup and sipped that. When she paid the check, she was almost the last person in the room.

Rain still fell. She could see it through the arched entrance of the lobby, dripping from the marquee and slanting steadily on the taxis, the wet street and the people hurrying under umbrellas. Her friend, the doorman, stood near the curb with his giant umbrella, and she watched him for a while as he opened the doors of the cars and helped people in and out. Occasionally he blew his whistle, and a taxi would come sloshing and grinding amid a rattle of shouts.

Loitering at the head of the stairs, she cocked her spectacles at the rain as though she, too, were about to order a taxi or was waiting for the rain to slacken like the group inside the entrance. The group kept changing, though, and after one man had stood there as long as she and had turned around twice, Eppy retired to the lobby.

She strolled toward the stands where theatre tickets, books and magazines were sold. There was a big board with the names of shows on it, and Eppy read them all several times. She read the titles of the books and pored over the covers of the magazines.

"Anything I can do for you?"

"No, thank you."

Then, because the girl did not move away but remained across the counter from her, Eppy said, "I'd like a paper."

She tucked the paper under one arm, crossed the lobby, entered the elevator, gave the number of her floor, got out and found the right corridor. After she had put the key in the latch, she hesitated. Then, with a wrench, she flung open the door, staring around her from the threshold. Everything in the room was the same.

Eppy took off her hat and seated herself in the easy chair. The paper lay unopened in her lap. She looked at her watch. It was ten minutes past two. She had been up nearly eight hours, yet the day was not half over. Suddenly she began to tremble, holding onto the arms of the chair and staring straight ahead of her.

She shook all over. Her legs shook and her teeth. Her feet jerked on the carpet. She could not stop them. She could only hold onto the arms while the rest of her body went to pieces and water ran soundlessly out of her eyes and the room around her became a yellow wash.

Like advancing monsters in the haze she saw them: her father as he pushed across his desk the check for a thousand dollars; her mother with those imploring yet horribly eager eyes; her brothers and her sister and her friends, the girls at the library and the girls at Sister Craycraft's. She saw the announcement cards that had been engraved and probably mailed by now. She saw her picture they said they were going to put in the paper. She saw the gifts, the telegrams, the letters. And persons she had never seen came grinning through the haze with the aunts and uncles and cousins thrice removed—grinning, fawning, skeptical—and Eppy cowered, the water dribbling down her cheeks and a sound coming now, a whimper in a high, fixed key far back in her twittering throat.

The whimper went on when the tears had ceased. She would wipe her eyes and blow her nose, for a while she would be dry of tears and free of shaking—and the whimper would come in a strangling bleat. She did not fight it. She let the whimper rock her with the regularity of hiccoughs, sitting there inert but for the twitch of her neck and the high, sad cry.

There happened to her at last, more as a phantom pointing than any inner impulse, some recognition of her plight. She could not sit whimpering in that room forever. She must go out to the world, now or later, else the world would batter in to her. What she was to do when she passed that door, she could grasp no more tangibly than she could the young god of that myth that had lived only in her fancy. She knew only that she must slay the god yet leave the world undoubting his divinity. She must, somehow, save herself.

Here she actually tried to consider a way out. Confession she rejected with a repugnance close to panic. To retrace a step down that proud road was impossible. But to go on was to go as the hunted thief, the shadow of discovery forever at her side. She could not go on. The end of the road was here, in this room.

If he who had never lived had died, she thought, then I would have their sympathy, their pity, instead of their ridicule and scorn. I can say he died. ... But what is death, without the dead, save a myth?

She opened the newspaper and spread it across her knees. Absently her eyes went down the page. At the foot of a column, at an item with a single line above it, they stopped. The whimper ceased. Into Eppy's swollen face crept a look of queer, childlike cunning.

3

Detective Sergeant Joe McGinley, being a man of small mind in a position of some authority, viewed his job weightily and himself with ceaseless, wholehearted admiration. In to him, at his desk in a room desolate as a sand-spit, blew the nameless dust of a great city, and with it a horde of the living who sought among these fragments the forsaken and the lost. Some came to the morgue who were high in office, enlisting the Sergeant's help in matters of major crime. Most hoped yet dreaded to find the face that would wring merely a family. One and all Sergeant McGinley received majestically. But the eminent—ranking officers, medical examiners, often the Commissioner himself—he received also with respect.

"Them birds, them reg'lar body-snatchers," Sergeant McGinley was accustomed to expound, "they gimme a pain. They look at a pitcher and they say, 'Yes, that's him, that's poor old Bill, I reco'nize him by his han'some nose,' or his dear eyes, or some'n. And I say to 'em, 'You're sure that's Bill?' and they says,

'Oh, yes, it couldn't possibly be nobody but Bill, exactly like I seen him last week,' and that's when I says, 'Sorry, sister, but you must notta known Bill so good. That's a pitcher of Neill Cream. He was hanged in England in 1893. You wasn't no relative of his, was you?' "

"I gotta be always on the k'veevy," Sergeant McGinley would explain, "or them phony widders would steal the stiffs right out from under me. Hoping they's insurance, y'know."

And Sergeant McGinley, if he was in his office, as he was eight hours of the day, would produce the decoy photograph of Neill Cream and waggle his head as he shuffled it, like a marked card, among the photographs of the unidentified and unclaimed, most of them long since rotting up the River in the trenches of Hart's Island.

But for all his vigilance in behalf of the taxpayers and the insurance companies, Sergeant McGinley had his spot of chivalry. The average stranger walking into his presence got no more courtesy than the strangers rolling in on wheels. If, however, the stranger was a woman, and if Sergeant McGinley judged her a lady, he thawed. For Sergeant McGinley, as he would have informed you without waiting for you to discover it, was a gentleman and handsomely could give a lady her due.

The stranger who stood on his threshold that rainy November afternoon touched the gentleman McGinley at once. She was not, he acknowledged to the examiner's clerk afterward, so hot to look at. A dumpy, red-cheeked little woman, not young and not very old. Blinking at him through heavy spectacles. Clutching an umbrella which left streaks and puddles on the rough floor. It had been raining since dawn, and gusts of rain still beat against the windows in the twilight.

The Sergeant was alone. He had just dismissed a pest of East Side Jews whose wailing for one Yascha he had checkmated by leading them, through a series of devious questions, to identify a negro's corpse. He was about to close his big book and, with satisfaction, to call it a day, when he became aware of his caller.

"Well?" rapped the Sergeant, brusquely.

Her voice was the tipoff—"one of them blurry voices like she had a mouthful of mush. 'Is this the Mawgue?' she says, and I couldn't hardly understand her. I had to ask her to repeat herself. But I knowed right off she was Southern and a lady."

The Sergeant said this was the Morgue and what could he do for her, and the woman, still timorous in the doorway, said something so low and slurred that the Sergeant cupped his ear and again asked her to repeat herself. She told him that she was hunting for her fiancé, who was missing.

The Sergeant bade her approach, and when she had done so and laid on his desk under its hard light, a newspaper clipping, he recognized it as referring to the floater fished that morning from the East River.

But that, he assured her, could not be her fiancé—the Sergeant pronounced it "your fie-ancy"—that was a bum.

The woman blinked and the Sergeant said, "Alcoholic case. He was just a bum, lady. He'd been drinking too much smoke and fell off."

The woman blinked resolutely.

"My fiancé," she said, "smoked and drank."

So the Sergeant opened the book, flipped a page or two and asked her a question. How old was he, how tall and what did he weigh? The woman, he observed, began to tremble. She said, in her sloshy, yet captivating voice, that he was a man of middle age, that he was of medium height and that she was not sure what he weighed—a hundred and fifty? a hundred and eighty? how could you tell what folks weighed just by looking at them? The Sergeant frowned. His record gave the floater's age as forty-five, his height as five feet six, and his weight one hundred and forty pounds.

"What kind of clothes was he wearing when you seen him last?"

The floater had had on blue pants and a brown coat, in the pockets of which were nothing but tobacco crumbs and thirty-five cents. The Sergeant waited.

But the woman, now, was shaking so that he got up and told her to take his chair, and this she did, gripping the arms and blinking up at him with such scared, desperate eyes, that he forgot his question and demanded, with what was kindness in McGinley, why she had come there all alone.

She then explained that her home was "down South" and she had arrived in New York only that morning. Her fiancé, who also lived out of town, was to meet her at the train, but when he appeared neither there nor at her hotel, she had telephoned his home, where the startled servants—he was a bachelor with no living relatives what ever—stated he had left the night before for New York. More worried than ever, she was distractedly reading the newspaper when she stumbled on the item that sent her, frantic, to the Morgue. For the man in the item had only three fingers on his left hand, and her fiancé's left hand had had only three fingers. The fourth, she said, had been cut off in an accident in his youth.

Her piteous gaze seemed to accuse the Sergeant of performing the amputation. This dame was a lady—but she was dumb.

"Well," he said. "It very likely ain't him. Don't let that scare you, lady. Floaters rot. They might easy rot off a finger. Any scars or incriminatin' marks on his body?"

The Sergeant immediately regretted the question, for his lady had gone bright pink.

"I—don't know!" she choked.

The Sergeant coughed. A gentleman should have had more sense than to ask that.

"Well, look here." He turned to his book and, unnerved by chagrin and that fact that the woman had begun to weep, broke an old McGinley rule. He read aloud from the record. At the end he declaimed, "Now, that don't sound like him, does it?"

"It might be!" she sobbed.

Her foggy spectacles besought the Sergeant.

"Can I see him? Oh, I can tell in a minute if I can only see him!"

The Sergeant said, "Well, I dunno, it's irregular."

He stared at her dubiously. Her hands picked at her quivering mouth.

"Was he insured?" he demanded.

The woman's head shook violently.

She cried, "I was all he had in the world!—he was all I had!"

Sentiment oozed under the McGinley ribs. Her grief oddly pleased him. He felt paternal, and not averse to prolonging the feeling.

"Y'see, lady, we gotta be careful. I always gotta be on the k'veevy—you'd be surprised at them that claims corpses for what they can make out of 'em. Most the unidentifieds been dead months, years, buried up there on the Island. But we got pitchers of 'em all, front and profile, and ain't a day somebody don't come in here wit' a phony claim. After the insurance, y'know. But I got a little stunt to stop *that!* Now your case, that's different. We ain't had time to take no pitcher and, besides, we still got the body. I'll show it to you, lady, and if you identify it and this corpse ain't got no other next of kin and you want to save the city of New York the expense of interment—"

"Oh, yes!" interrupted the woman. "Oh, yes, I do!"

"Well, come along," said the Sergeant. "Don't let it scare you, lady—it was an autopsy case and they most generally clean them up."

A cold wind blew along the corridor they entered, the Sergeant thumping ahead and the woman skuttling close to him with short, hurrying steps. But the head of the stairs broke the wind, and as they descended by an iron rail on one side and a white wall on the other, it was like descending into a vacuum. Nothing came up to them save light and silence and static layers of air, which only the overwrought would snuff in fearful fancy.

A gnarled man, stooped over a pile of sacks that looked like lime, regarded them through hair unkempt across his forehead.

"Four forty-six," said the Sergeant.

They traversed another corridor and were in a chamber opening suddenly. The room was all stone floor and walls, but in the wall, as high as a man could reach and as low as his ankles, were rows of doors like the closed doors of safes. They were fairly large, a yellowish brown color, and each had a lever like the handle of a refrigerator.

"Four forty-six," repeated the gnarled man.

The Sergeant followed him across the room and put his hand on one of the levers.

"Here y'are, lady."

He sank his weight, the door swung, and out to the three flowed a tongue of icy air. With it trundled, on rollers, a long, deep tray.

"This side, lady."

The front of the tray was high, too high to peer over from where she stood, and she had not realized, until she moved, that the corpse had come out feet last. She saw first the swathed legs, then, half turning, the head at her very shoulder, propped on its metal pillow face up.

She shrieked.

"No—no! no!—I can't! I can't!"

Cringing, holding her hands against her eyes, she heard the tray rumble, heard the thud of the door and the lever's click, and pressed her fingers tighter and shook her head back and forth.

The Sergeant said, "Not him, lady?"

She moaned. She mumbled something like "no."

"Well, I gotta confess I tricked you." The Sergeant rubbed palm on palm. "I gotta admit that's the wrong guy, lady. Y'see, we gotta be careful." He included the gnarled man in his exposition.

"The rule is go slow. That's the Commissioner's rule and that's my rule. I've seen 'em fall for that plant when they had me foxed right up to the ice box. But I guess you ain't foolin'. Jed—roll out four thirty-two."

The Sergeant, still massaging his palms, walked after Jed. For a moment the figure of the woman held its cramped posture, like that of a plump bolster driven into itself. Then, had the Sergeant turned, he would have seen her hands come away from the eyes, her head lift and over her face settle a look so fixed that a sculptor's fist might have clapped it there. Desperation was in it and a kind of stark courage.

She stood staring down for several minutes.

"That's Jocelyn Randolph," she said.

The Sergeant had seen them go cold like that—cold and staring as they thrust the tray back, walking away too stunned to speak and, upstairs in the medical examiner's office, giving the dope to the clerk as calm as you please. Only once, after the certificate was made out and they told her she must wait seventy-two hours in a case where the claimant was not blood kin, did that wild fright spring again into her eyes and her wrists begin to shake.

"But don't let that worry you, Miss Spurlock," said the Sergeant. "You go ahead and notify your undertaker, he'll fix all that."

"I don't know an undertaker!"

The Sergeant grinned. "Well, I can't help you there. Strictly against the rules. But Frank here"—he winked at Frank—"I guess Frank will be glad to 'phone somebody, eh, Frank?"

The Sergeant escorted Miss Spurlock to the street and whistled for a taxi and helped her into it. His paternal glow defied the rain.

"She's a real little Southern lady," he informed the examiner's clerk. "By God, I almost ast her to come again!"

They roared, their mirth bellowing gargantuan down the windy halls.

"Well, that's three to-day we saved the City," said the Sergeant, "and your cut from O'Connor. It's about time I blowed. See you in the funny paper, Frank!"

CHAPTER FOURTEEN

O N Monday, November seventeenth, just a week since she had informed the world of her engagement and the morning after she left Corinth to meet her lover, the local newspapers announced in their society columns the marriage of Miss Eppy Gordon Spurlock to Mr. Jocelyn Randolph in New York City.

On Tuesday they amended this statement with the story on their front pages of Mr. Randolph's death by accidental drowning on his wedding eve. The tragic news, they said, came in a telegram to the family. "Miss Spurlock, who was prostrated, is bringing the remains here for burial."

For a day the family enjoyed public sympathy and behaved with proper, and genuine, regret. A few of Eppy's friends, Nancy Bergo among them, ached for her.

On Friday, a hand opened the retort of a Long Island crematory, brushed the ridge of ash into a pan and tilted this above a bronze urn on which the hand deftly screwed a lid.

That night Eppy Spurlock boarded a train for the South, refusing her redcap's aid with the bundle he assured the porter must be good stuff.

That night, too, in a speakeasy in Greenwich Village, Eloise King laughed for no apparent reason. To the man with her she said she had suddenly remembered something she'd been trying to remember. "And, oh, won't I tell it to a certain bunch I know!" Next day she wrote three letters.

On Monday, the twenty-fourth, Major Wallace MacArthur, adjusting a black cravat before his mirror, sighed over man's eternal genuflections to the Dark Angel.

Funerals, mused the Major, were getting entirely too frequent in a life he had long ago pledged to Dionysos. The hours he had wasted in drafty churches and wet cemeteries made him wish he had been born Irish, who at least drank their dead into golgotha. Time was when he had rather relished funerals. The fine old hymns soothed, the phrases of th burial service—which he could chant with any preacher—gave death a noble beauty. But in the last few years funerals had begun to chafe him. They were too many. He could not pick up a newspaper without encountering a familiar name in the obituaries, he could scarcely answer a telephone without becoming an honorary escort.

"Always a pall-bearer, never a corpse," the Major muttered sardonically into his mustaches.

It was depressing enough when the members of his own generation dropped fast; what right had these younger ones to summon him to lamentation? He had frozen patiently last week while the red earth gaped for Peter Block's sarcophagus (he and Peter had rocked niggers together in 1875), and his knuckles on the silver grips had not protested the heaviness of Mrs. General Sholto, who had been so frail a girl. Even his attendance at Mrs. Craycraft's funeral he had bestowed willingly, blowing his nose during the requiem as he thought of her, waltzing lightly in his arms. But his fortitude cracked when the deceased was a stranger and a half-Yankee to boot.

"You've got to go," Nancy had said, "because Tony won't. You know how he is about those things—even Mammy wringing a chicken's neck."

"But I don't know Miss Spurlock and I didn't know her intended—it would be presumptuous of me," declared the Major.

"Presumptuous rubbish! You mean you'd rather be somewhere else at five o'clock, holding services over dead soldiers. You know Eppy's father—I heard you say you did. Besides, I'm not going alone. I want you with me to cheer me up. I've had enough horrors lately."

"Well, I've had enough funerals to last me a—"

"You'd go if you'd seen her," interrupted Nancy. Her gaze became pensive. "I wish you'd been with me this afternoon. I admit I wouldn't have dreamed of going to the house if she hadn't telephoned. But now I'm glad I did. She hasn't any friends, Dad. And that family! I think she needed somebody. To stand between her and them. Somebody who wasn't so damn related to her!

"They were all sitting around when I got there. Papa and Mamma and that dumb brother, and a younger brother, and Sara Lee, who isn't so bad. They were in the parlor, the shades were down like the funeral had started already, and they were trying so hard to look sad and sympathetic. Having a tough time doing it, too, I guess. I bet if they'd said what they thought, it would have been one big squawk—no millionaire brother-in-law and Eppy back on their hands.

"Well, there she was, off the train just the night before, and pretty straggly looking. She looks pretty straggly most of the time, of course, but with all of them staring at her, she looked stragglier than usual. She was sitting on the piano stool in the middle of 'em with those fat legs just touching the floor and her skirt all humpy and her hair a mess and those specs down on her nose, and at first I thought, my God! they might give her a comfortable chair, anyway. Arid then I saw it on the end of the piano—Eppy wasn't going to budge an inch farther away from it than she had to."

"It?" said the Major. "It?"

"The urn. She had him cremated, you know, and she brought the ashes back with her. That's what they're holding the services for this afternoon—ashes in an urn."

"Good God!" said the Major.

"Well, she wanted it that way and it seems it's not such an uncommon thing. Plenty of people cremate and I guess they can have the funeral after the cremation as well as before. Anyway, all that was left of Eppy's romance was in that pot and you knew without looking at her what was in her face whenever she'd take a swing on the stool. I looked once and I didn't want to look again.

"And then I began to get it. I don't know exactly what they'd been saying to her, but I could guess by the way old Spurlock hemmed and hawed and beat around the bush. They were wondering about the money. Only they didn't quite have the courage to come right out and ask her.

"She'd written them, you see, that Jocelyn had no surviving relatives, that's why she was taking charge of the body; it hadn't occurred to them before to even wonder about Jocelyn's family—careful who Eppy married, weren't they?—but now it was the most important thing in the world; a million dollars might be parked on the piano stool and they weren't taking any chances of offending it. I don't think the Spurlocks were awfully glad to see me.

"But Eppy was. She hopped down and kissed me and cried a little, and I never was so sorry for anybody in my life, until I began to get it some more.

"She did the talking. You know how it is, generally, when people lose some one they love? They don't say much and it's awful. I'd heard Eppy on the subject of Jocelyn and I figured this was going to be pretty awful, too. But it wasn't. You didn't have to rack your brain for something to say—she said it first; you didn't have to put your arms around her and say 'there, there!'—after those first tears she didn't shed a drop.

"She said—Lord, Dad, I can't begin to tell you what she said! Except it was exactly the sort of stuff you'd expect from a widow still keeping his memory green after forty years. You know what I mean?—devotion?—loyalty?—'I will never desert Mr. Micawber'?"

"I know," said the Major.

"It wasn't funny, Dad. I don't mean to make fun of her. I can see what it's going to be the rest of her life—living her only romance over and over—the letters laid away in lavender—his picture—probably the urn in a shrine in her bedroom. Yet, in a way, I'm glad. Glad that chap died. Eppy didn't know a blessed thing about sex. He might have made her completely miserable."

"She doesn't sound broken-hearted," remarked the Major.

"She's not. That's what got the family's goat. If she'd wept, collapsed, but she didn't—and they didn't know what to do. They just sat and mooned at her while she ran on about eternal life and love stronger than the grave and Jocelyn's spirit near her, and every now and then she'd cut an eye at that urn, and it was weird!"

"The woman's crazy," said the Major. "A ouija board is all she needs."

"Sure she's crazy, but she's pretty cute about it. She had the family buffaloed all right. They couldn't drag up vulgar money while she was raving about her holy love for the man."

"Do you really think he left her a fortune?"

"Wait—I'm coming to that. I'd been there nearly an hour and Eppy hadn't stopped to draw breath. She was addressing all her remarks to me—I tell you she was relieved to have somebody else around—and I was just nodding and saying 'yes' and the family hadn't gotten to first base. And then little brother spilled the beans.

"I dare say he was getting restive. Shut up in a parlor on a bright Sunday afternoon and the other kids raising the devil. We could hear them yelling outside every once in a while. Finally, he couldn't stand it any longer.

" 'Say, Eppy,' he said, 'you gonna get a car now? Say, get a Hispano-Suiza, will you?'

"She just blinked at him. I'm willing to bet she hadn't the faintest idea what was coming.

" 'A car?' she said.

" 'Sure,' said Bubber, 'Mr. Randolph left you all his jack, didn't he?'

"Well, it was awful. You could have heard a pin drop. I could have killed that boy, but they didn't do a thing to him, didn't even look at him, they were in such a fever to get the glad tidings. They looked at Eppy like a lot of dogs looking at a bone. She'd gone every color from red to white. For a minute she didn't say a thing—it was almost like she didn't know what to say—and then she just knocked them cold.

" 'Didn't I write you?' she chirped. 'Why, Jocelyn didn't leave me anything. He lost all his money in Wall Street. That's why he drowned himself. He couldn't bear to come to me a bankrupt!'

"That finished 'em. Maybe they knew it before—about his drowning himself, I mean—and didn't tell the papers, but the stuff about the money was news. You could see that. And you know, I had the funniest feeling that she made it up right there. But if she did, that didn't do the family any good. They believed her. What else could they do? And they were sunk—all but Sara Lee. Sara Lee was a little brick. She jumped up and patted Eppy on the back. 'Don't you mind, Eps, we'll take care of you,' she said, and then Eppy did bawl."

The Major shook his head.

"I give it up," he said. "It's unnatural, that's what it is. All these youngsters killing themselves. And that urn business—chucking 'em in the fire like so many roasting ears."

"Well, I'm not asking you to his cremation," Nancy said.

"Oh, I'll go," he groaned. "But I don't like it. When my time comes, Nancy—no urns. I won't have it! The human body deserves a better end than a five-cent cigar."

He still did not like it this morning, when the world beyond his windows called a truce to sorrow. Autumn lay splendid and rejuvenating upon the earth. Out there where the woods flamed and the wind sowed the fields with the next harvest, there should be no dank tombs and wailing caravans, there should be a nigger and a hound in the creek bottom, tallyho across the hills, and a bumper at the run's end for the laughing heart. Let the dead bury their dead, thought the Major. And, glimpsing his son-in-law striding hatless across a lawn still rich with green, he hurried down to intercept him in the hall.

"Chief, good morning!—What's the good word?"

"Do a fellow a favor, will you, Tony? Take Nancy to that funeral to-day like a good chap."

Shaved to the blood, pink from the frosty air—the antithesis of everything funereal—Tony regarded him with reproach. Then his face lightened, he shifted to his left hand the morning paper and the mail.

"Don't," said the Major, "you can't bribe me."

"Be yourself, Chief. What kind of a guy do you think I am? I'll match you—heads or tails—"

"Heads," said the Major. He straightened with a grunt. "Doggone you, Tony—you have hell's own luck!"

But breakfast restored him. Eating!—life's first and last pleasure—what man can cavil who boasts teeth, belly and that with which to put them to work? And to-day Mammy had cooked scrapple, which the Major loved. The sun struck valiantly across the table, Skeet entered with a coffee pot steaming, and the Major laid to with brief but hearty thanks to heaven.

Tony, who had dropped Nancy's mail beside her empty plate and was opening his own, provided a further whip to gloom. This was a letter he tossed over without a word.

The Major chortled.

"N S F, eh? The little skunk! But what a nerve he has to let it bounce back from his own bank! Practically daring you to collect, son."

"Maybe it's a mistake. Maybe he didn't know he was overdrawn."

"Bosh—he simply takes you for an easy mark—let me keep this check."

"Okay, Chief. But under your hat—see? I mean Nancy. Fact is, between me and you, I let Prentiss have another case."

The Major surveyed his son-in-law with disgust, remarked that the fine weather had gone to his head, and pocketed the check as Nancy entered.

"Hi, family," she said. "How're the Rollo boys?"

They had risen together, the Major swallowing and Tony fumbling at her chair, and she smiled because they were both a little clumsy in their gallantry, the one from too long practice and the other from not enough, and because she would not have had either otherwise. They were, she told them—and they could take it as they pleased—a precious pair.

While she read her mail, the Major talked. Real estate, he informed Tony, was at the bottom of the bottom, there was never a worse time to get money out or a better to put money in. And Tony, guilty over that check, listened eagerly. He was glad that they three were alone for once and that it would not be long, now, before drunks at breakfast would be merely a social adjunct, not a business necessity, and he could shower Nancy with the fruits of legitimate commerce instead of hiding from her the phony transactions of an outlawed traffic.

"Frozen assets—sure they are," said the Major. "But if you've got the cash, freeze to 'em."

He suspended his fork, curiosity suddenly alert.

"What's the letter, daughter? You're mighty interested. No more funerals, I trust?"

Nancy looked up; looked from one to the other. "It's from Eloise King. Isn't that strange? Why should she write to me? But that isn't the strangest thing…it's what she says…about Eppy Spurlock.…"

They watched her read on, turn a page and read on to the end.

"Well?" said the Major.

She shook her head.

"I don't understand. If what she says is true—and I'm scared it is—after all, I had a hunch from the first—"

"What's true?" urged the Major.

Nancy struck her hands together.

"But if it's so—good Lord!—then who—what—is in that thing?"

She gazed at them in frank horror.

"Look here," said the Major, "can't you talk sense? It is a little odd, I grant you, that you should get a letter from that one—she didn't shine up to you for sour apples—but I still don't see any deep mystery—"

"Oh, hush a minute! It's obvious why she wrote. She simply wanted to spread gossip—to be malicious—hurt somebody—anybody! I guess she didn't love us awfully much when she left here and—by Jinks!—I bet she wrote others, too, Sally and heavens knows who. But that's immaterial. It's what she says about Eppy that gets me!"

"Well, what *does* she say?" cried her exasperated father.

"She says this." Nancy's eyes went to the letter and returned to them, dark and foreboding. "She rode up on the same train with Eppy. Eppy raved about her sweetheart. She showed Eloise his picture. And Eloise says there is no such man in New York as Jocelyn Randolph. She tried to look him up. And she says, furthermore, that she recognized the picture. It's another man's, she says, a radio singer named Lou Harris who gives away his photograph to anybody who writes for it. She says, 'I heard Lou Harris on the air last night.' And she wrote this letter the day after Eppy left New York with that urn!"

2

At ten o'clock, with breakfast over an hour, they had decided nothing, and when, at three, the Major returned from a scouting trip to town, they were no nearer a solution or a program of action.

"All quiet along the Potomac," he announced. "Newspapers ... police ... undertakers ... the Spurlock family ... if anybody but us in this town smells a nigger in the woodpile, I don't know who it is!"

The council of strategy had assembled in the living-room, where Nancy presided and Tony guarded the door in case Mammy Pickett asserted her rights as a member of the family. The Major, center of interest, spoke from an easy chair. His appearance was as unruffled as ever, but dew dampened his temples, and his throat, he would have declaimed to the multitudes, was like a powder horn.

"I went to Waveroon's first," he said. "Old Waveroon likes nothing better than a good, ghastly chat about his latest prize, and he was easy to pump. Everything shipshape there. I even saw the death certificate. Then I drifted around to the newspaper offices. Not a ripple. Same with the police and the coroner. So I tried old Spurlock. He hadn't seen me in twenty years, but he's just pompous enough to believe my sympathetic interest was natural. You can tell he's still pretty riled over the money, but I'm sure he hasn't heard anything more. Let me infer that his daughter was coming into a considerable sum. I don't doubt the old boy intends to keep that business dark and maybe float a loan on the strength of the fabulous Randolph millions."

The Major wiped his forehead and his nose.

"Well," he added, "that's my story. Now you tell."

Nancy told. She had 'phoned Eppy. She had talked to Eppy and Sara Lee both. If either had received any upsetting news in the mail, neither their manner nor their words showed it.

"But," said Nancy, "somebody else did get a letter."

The Major's gaze questioned.

"Sally Chapman," said Nancy.

The Major sighed. His morning's work for nothing. If he knew anything about women, Eloise King's bombshell would shortly pepper the town.

"I drove over there," said Nancy. "You know, we'd forgotten to return that vanity case she left and it was a good excuse. It was the first time I'd seen Sally or any of that crowd since Sister's death and we had quite a talk. I'm sorry for Sally, she and Sister were such pals. She wasn't only cut up a lot, but she seems lonely now. She wanted to know if I'd take up tap-dancing with her. Imagine! I hope I'm not that fat! Well, she knew I knew what really happened about Sister—it might as well have been in the papers the way gossip travels in Corinth—and she let out some more I didn't know. Sally isn't very smart. It was about Eloise and Howard."

The Major had a quick flash of Howard as Howard had looked at the funeral, a sad young man he had liked once, and struck once, and somehow could not pity even in his grief.

"Go ahead," he said, "what about the letter?"

"I'm coming to that. What she told me really leads up to it. I don't want to start a scandal, but the fact is Sally lays most of the blame for Sister's suicide on Eloise. Something Howard said that night. Anyway, there's no love lost there; if Sally didn't exactly put Eloise out of her house, she certainly wasn't sorry to see her go. And so—here's the point—when she got a letter from Eloise this morning, she tore it up without reading it!"

"Noble!" The Major slapped his leg. "That's two down."

He hesitated, his eyes watered in Tony's direction, then his impulse proved irresistible.

"There was a third letter," he announced.

"There was? Why, Pop, you old cheater, were you going to hold out on me?"

Somewhat sheepishly, the Major withdrew an envelope from his pocket and, while she read, while he twisted his mustaches in pride and defiance, he recalled with keen satisfaction his moment in the bank. It had been pretty smart of him to remember Prentiss with everything else he'd had to think of, and smarter still to ransom the letter after he'd discovered it. What, if anything, Prentiss had intended to do with it, he was not sure, but he knew the letter was as safe from exposure now as the bad check still buried in his wallet.

"How did you know he got one, too?" demanded Nancy.

The Major tapped his chest. "Old Cap Collier!"

"Well, how did you come into it?"

"Ah, there!" chuckled the Major.

In his corner, Tony sweated, eager to protect Eppy and out-jockey the other woman—eager for anything Nancy was for—but not unaware that he seemed headed for a tough break.

"What do you mean, 'ah there'? He'll tell it all over town."

"No," said the Major, "he won't. That young man, Nancy, is a very cowardly young man. And he has reasons to fear me. If you don't mind, I won't go into them. The story concerns none of us and the details are extremely—er—masculine. Let's have that document!"

And, with a wink for Tony, the Major rose, took Miss Eloise King's regrets that she could not attend Mr. Prentiss's tea-party, and dropped these, with their attendant gossip about Eppy Spurlock, into the fire.

"There—my advice is to do the same thing with yours. The damn woman seems to operate a regular correspondence school, but I've got a hunch she stopped with three. Do you think she wrote Craycraft?"

Nancy watched the green paper curl to black.

"No," she said, "she wouldn't write Howard. No woman could after what happened—not even Eloise."

"Good." The Major turned his back to the blaze, gently rubbing its warmth into his lean haunches. "Then that's that. And here we are, right back where we started from. The question before the house is, 'What are we going to do about it?' And I vote we do something." He paused. "Let's take a look at the whole business. We know—or we're pretty sure—that Miss Spurlock lied about her engagement from the first. She invented letters, picture, everything, possibly with a New York confederate, though I'll wager she was mighty cagey at that end, too. Well, who was hurt by it? Nobody. Eppy got a thrill and a few presents nobody begrudges her. You don't begrudge her that silver dingus, do you?"

"Certainly not!"

"All right. She was no worse than most women. I've seen 'em pretending at romance all my life, if it wasn't more than to say the laundry-driver flirted with 'em. Only Eppy seems to have been too blame good at pretending. She reached the point where it was put up or shut up. She had to make good and by George, she did! How, I don't know. I wish I did know. But whatever it was she did up there in New York—and crazy people are notoriously cunning—she appears to have gotten away with it handsomely! ... And I'm for her."

"Then you really think a man's ashes are in that urn?"

The Major made a face.

"Beans porridge hot, beans porridge cold, beans porridge in the pot—who knows? The record says so. From what you tell me, a lot of ghouls leave them lying around loose. Maybe she picked 'em up in somebody's drawing-room. And suppose they are some Northerner's—cold-blooded lot—not above peddling a pint of Aunt Sara's bones. I say, let Eppy keep 'em if she gets any fun out of 'em.

"Moreover," added the Major, "suppose they're not human ashes. Suppose they're cigar ashes. Or mud, plain mud. Are you going to spoil Eppy's romance on account of a little Yankee mud?"

"No," said Nancy, "I'm not."

She, too, got up.

"I'm glad you feel that way about it, Pop. That's how I feel. What do you say, Tony?"

"Me?" said her husband. "It ain't in my line, baby—body ashes. Whatever you and the Chief say, goes."

They regarded each other, three not unhappy conspirators.

"Then," said the Major, "let's get going. Tony, you'll drive us down, at least? So far as I'm concerned, we depart to attend the obsequies of Mr. Jocelyn Randolph, a gentleman I never met in the flesh but one whose demise, as the sweetheart of a home-town girl, I deplore. May his ashes rest in peace! And by the way, Nancy"—he patted again his warm spot—"wouldn't a little drink to the deceased be appropriate?"

She came over, taking his arm.

"You're an old fox, Major MacArthur—I thought all this industry and oratory were leading up to something. But, honey, can't you hold your horses till we get back? I promise you a *real* drink then. How about a regular, old-fashioned julep?"

And the Major, privately resolving to waylay Skeet at once, declared a julep after services was acceptable.

CHAPTER FIFTEEN

S o, in Waveroon's chapel, with its austere stained glass and its air of divine authority, they committed to God, looking for the general resurrection and the life of the world to come, the spirit of Eppy's stranger. Solemnly they craned their necks at the urn among the flowers, solemnly suffered the psalms and hymns, and solemnly they hid their curious stares while the minister prayed this corruptible into incorruption.

They did not make a large congregation. The Spurlocks, the Moons, the other relatives unto the cousins thrice re-removed. A few women from the neighborhood. The library girls. And Eppy herself, pudgy but erect under her black veil. Whether, behind it, she wept, they could not tell, seeing through their laced fingers that not even during the benediction did she bow. To the Major, watching her, came the fancy that her veil actually was white and she a bride and the music was not "Lead, Kindly Light" but the wedding march.

He sat in a rear pew with his daughter, musing on the insanities of this generation and the blind hand that had drawn together these childhood friends for a little while, to toss them about like keys in a pocket.

But yesterday, he remembered, they were youngsters, of the same age, a like ancestry, a common breeding and a destiny that appeared sure. They would be as their fathers were and do as their fathers did. ... Yet they are not as we were, he thought. They are at once harder and softer, stronger yet curiously weak. They dare all things and are satisfied by none. They go at life violently, yet how inevitably they seem to miss happiness! They are insatiable—one wonders they don't savor their pleasures a little longer before they snap at the next excitement. ...

What they need, he decided, is a few lessons in simple living. ... I should like, for example, to found a School of Drinking, co-educational, the graduates of which would be able to converse agreeably and intelligently after a final examination of cocktails, wines and an assortment of cordials and highballs after dinner. ... We should have to conscript a foreigner for dean, I suppose, but I should certainly occupy the Chair of Bourbon. ...

This picture was so pleasing to the Major that, to Nancy's horror, he chuckled.

Seriously, he contended with himself, these people live too hectically. Their liquor, their love affairs, their jobs, their recreations, they ride at them as hellbent as they went to war and as though infidelity, drunkenness, making money and squandering it were a form of patriotism. ... But I suppose the world itself is hectic. The world has changed, a whirligig to nowhere. Can you blame its inhabitants for going mad? ...

The Major's head began to nod. He shook it.

No—he reflected—the world is not so changeable nor so very bad. As good as it ever was or ever will be. And the people in it are probably no different from the apes or the angels. The human race has always been more than a little crazy; am I, a potential professor of Bacchus College, less a crackpot than that Spurlock girl, who hears Mendelssohn in a Methodist dirge, or that fellow in the black dickey, dreaming of stars in his crown?

"Wake up," said Nancy. "It's over. And what on earth were you grinning about? Any one would think you enjoyed funerals?"

"I do," said the Major.

Outside Tony waited with the car.

"Get in," said Nancy to her father, "and go to sleep. No—back there. I want to ride with the Boss."

The Major snorted as he always did when she said something that appealed to his sense of the ironic. At least, he reflected, she and Tony had pulled some sense out of this hurly-burly.

He did not go to sleep. The sun was cold in the red west and a cold wind blew, but he drew the laprobe close and hummed an old tune. ... "Weep no more, my lady, oh, weep no more today." And he saw, beyond the cold city, the bright land that had cradled him and his ... I am sorry for them, he thought, these Eppies and Sisters and ladies of to-day; I am sorry for all the children who came after us into the old land and the new time. Yet what faced them was no harsher, was it, than what faced the children of any land, of any time? "The sun also rises," says Ecclesiastes, and to-morrow the sun will come up again, over the red hills that I knew, the piney woods, the cotton fields. It will shine bright—on their tall buildings, the machines, the clamor and the speed, on still another generation shouting at the doors. But I shall not weep for any of them. I shall not weep for the land. And the Major repeated another verse from the Bible which said that a man had no better thing under the sun than to eat, and to drink, and to be merry. So, as a machine rushed him deeper into the land, he ceased to think at all, holding in his mind's eye the simple vision of a tall glass with a tuft of green and a sash of frost and a base of green and amber.